DEFIANCE

MASTERS OF THE SHADOWLANDS
BOOK 14

CHERISE SINCLAIR

VanScoy Publishing Group

Defiance
Copyright © 2018 by Cherise Sinclair
ISBN: 978-1-947219-11-3
Published by VanScoy Publishing Group
Cover Art: I'm No Angel Designs

DEDICATION

To Liz Berry because she told me to write this book.

ACKNOWLEDGMENTS

Hugs to Fiona Archer for the brainstorming...and the twist.

A huge thank you to Monette Michaels and Bianca Sommerland for critting this book and walloping me up alongside the head when the plot went astray.

For my beta readers: Y'all have no idea how much I appreciate you. Jennifer Foster for the amazing job of Alaska-proofing, (any errors are mine, not hers), Lisa White and Marian Shulman for spotting typos and grammar idiocies.

The Red Quill editors have once again pulled off a miracle at short notice. Y'all are simply fantastic.

AUTHOR'S NOTE

I took some liberties with the proximity of the JBER Base boundary to Fort Richardson National Cemetery. Writer's privilege, right?

The town of Rescue is all mine. Don't try to find it. <g>

CHAPTER ONE

"You know what an Irish wake is, Grayson?"

Sitting in his office, Zachary Grayson pulled in a deep, pained breath, not able to process the question. Because his old friend had cancer. *Cancer.*

And Mako was dying.

"Grayson?"

Grief thickened Zachary's voice. "Yes, Mako, I know what a wake is."

"Well, boy, my sons will handle the funeral, but would you do me a solid and set up a happy send-off for after? I don't want all the sitting with the body shit. Find a place with decent booze where whoever shows up can raise a glass and tell a few stories. Share the stupid shit I did when I was younger. So the boys can remember me alive and not in a box in the ground."

"I can do that." Zachary rubbed the sting from his eyes. *Dammit. Hold it back.* "I'll even tell one or two myself, First Sergeant. Maybe about how a bunch of streetwise foster children ended up in the wilds of Alaska."

As the raspy laugh rang through the phone, Zachary knew

that cancer might steal the sergeant's life, but death didn't frighten Mako. It never had.

"Good enough. My lawyer has your name and number. He'll contact you when the time comes." Mako's harsh voice went a degree softer. "It's been an honor to know you, Zachary. Thanks for looking out for the boys."

The silence said Mako had disconnected.

Dammit, Mako. Would Zachary ever hear his voice again?

Setting the phone down, he rested his eyes on a tranquil scene of white-capped Alaska mountains and forest, a painting he'd purchased when visiting his friend.

He had a feeling he'd be hearing from Mako's lawyer soon. Aching inside, he murmured the old Irish blessing. "Until we meet again, may God hold you in the hollow of his hand."

Pushing away from the desk, he glanced at the time. Almost five. He kept Mondays light, so there were no more counseling appointments today, and he had a need to hold his wife and daughter.

Out in the waiting room he shared with two other psychologists, Mrs. Ward smiled at him. Tactful, yet firm, she reminded him of his favorite grandmother. "Done for the day, Dr. Grayson?"

"Yes. I'll finish my paperwork at home so Sophia can keep me company." Not that he got much accomplished when she did.

Having met his eighteen-month-old despot, Mrs. Ward laughed.

"Is there anything urgent in the mail I should deal with tonight?"

"Here you go. I already removed the junk mail." Mrs. Ward handed him a stack.

Zachary glanced through the letters and tossed most into his in-basket for tomorrow. Since former patients often sent news of their progress, he opened the letter with a hand-printed address.

And froze.

"Dr. Grayson? Zachary? Is something wrong?"

"In a manner of speaking, yes." Silently, he read the letter again.

You arrogant asshole, you'll pay for what you did.

One bullet should do it.

"I seem to have received my first death threat."

"That's..." Mrs. Ward realized he wasn't joking, and her face went pale. "The police. You have to notify the police."

"I'll stop by there now." The local station wasn't far, and clients here might react badly to an influx of police. It would be best to visit them.

Careful not to add new fingerprints, he tucked everything into a manila envelope.

A minute later, he stepped out of the air-conditioned building into the hot humid air of early October in Tampa. A thunderstorm was just breaking over the city. As thunder echoed off the buildings, fat raindrops splattered on the cars in the parking lot.

Terrified at the cracks of thunder, a little five-year-old boy, a patient of Zachary's associate, huddled next to the building, ignoring the rain.

"Calm down. It's just thunder, Cody." His mother's attempts to get him moving sent him further into a ball.

"He's not having a good day, is he?" Zachary stopped next to her.

"Dr. Grayson. Hello."

"He'll do better inside and out of the noise. May I pick him up?"

She let out an exasperated breath. "Please."

Putting his own worries to one side, he touched the boy on the shoulder, projecting calm. "I'm going to pick you up, and we'll go inside where it's quieter."

When the boy didn't react, Zachary simply scooped him up, waited for the mother to open the door, and walked back inside. The lobby, decorated in calming blues and greens, had comfortable chairs lining the tall windows.

"Take a seat, please," he told the mother, and when she complied, he set Cody in her lap.

"There. This isn't as noisy, is it?" Dropping down on one knee to be level with the child, he smiled at the mother. "At his age, it's normal to be frightened of our loud Tampa storms. There are techniques that will help. Ask your counselor, or even look online."

"I shouldn't have been so impatient." She hugged her son. "We just moved here from Seattle, and we're used to nice quiet drizzles. These thunderstorms scare me, too."

"There will come a time you'll both enjoy the noise and light shows." Zachary patted her hand before searching through his pants pockets. He usually had something tucked away, depending on which little patients he'd seen during the day.

Ah, yes. He and one little girl had been blowing bubbles this morning. He pulled out the bottle. "Cody."

The boy's head rose just enough to reveal big brown eyes. Excellent. The fear had receded enough to allow the child's natural curiosity to awaken.

"I have a job for you." Pulling out the plastic ring, he blew a big bubble.

When it landed on Cody's knee and burst, the boy's eyes widened. And his lips curved up.

Almost there.

Zachary held up the ring again. "Every time a bubble comes close, I need you to take a big breath and blow it away."

As Cody wiggled to sit up, Zachary dropped his voice in a pseudo-warning. "If it lands on you, you lose a point. Are you up to the job?"

"I can do it!"

Zachary blew a bubble toward him, and the boy puffed hard to chase the bubble away.

"Wonderful work. Do it again." Another bubble. Another success.

And the thunderstorm was forgotten.

Looking up, Zachary met the mother's gaze. "Moving somewhere quieter and providing a diversion will usually work. Bubbles have the added benefit of requiring deep breathing, which is calming in itself."

Her face thoughtful, she nodded slowly. "He has a right to be scared, and I over-reacted. I'll do better next time."

"That's the spirit." Zachary blew another bubble and laughed when Cody puffed it up and into the air. "Good job."

After handing the bottle to the mother, he said, "The storm should move on within a few minutes. Have fun."

"Thank you." Her eyes glimmered briefly with tears as she hugged her son. "You turned a fight into fun. Thank you so much."

"You're quite welcome."

At the door, Zachary stopped. A death threat. Someone wanted to kill him. Although most threats tended to be someone letting off steam, this sender had sounded serious.

A signature would certainly have been useful. He couldn't think of anyone who held that much anger toward him.

As Zachary stepped outside, he glanced around. No one was pointing a rifle at him. Other people who worked in the building were leaving, hurrying to escape the downpour. Two cars rolled past. Lightning flashed, and a second later, thunder rumbled across the heavens.

Pulling up his collar against the rain, he strode quickly down the slope to his car, conveniently close. The parking space was one of the perks of owning the building.

As he crossed in front of his car, the hair on the back of his neck rose. He spun in a quick circle.

There. The man stood, half-hidden, in the tall firebush hedge at the building's side. The posture was unmistakable. He held a pistol pointed at Zachary.

Zachary lunged to the left.

5

The handgun barked, almost drowned out by a sizzling crack of lightning.

A streak of pain ripped across Zachary's upper arm as he dove between the two parked cars.

Another shot sounded, this one louder.

Heart hammering, he pulled out his phone and looked around the front of the car.

The shadow by the building had disappeared.

Shaken, Zachary closed his eyes and exhaled slowly. That had been far too close. He took two more breaths before doing a quick self-assessment. He had a rip in his shirtsleeve and a bleeding gouge high on his deltoid that stung like hell.

A chill ran cold fingers up his spine. If he hadn't moved, the bullet would have gone through his chest.

Rising, he spotted a hole in his front windshield where the second bullet had passed. Good, he'd have some evidence for the police.

More than just a bloody arm. Frowning at the blood, he opened the back door and picked up the paper towels beside Sophia's car seat.

And he froze in horror.

After passing through the windshield, the bullet had gone through the front seat and splintered the top edge of the car seat. If his daughter had been with him...

Like Mako, he was no stranger to death. But this...no man was prepared for this.

Fear for his family rose up within him like a tsunami.

———

That evening, Jessica Grayson carried her sleeping daughter into the nursery and laid her down in the crib. Smiling, she smoothed fluffy blonde hair off Sophia's rounded cheek. "Look how big you are now," she whispered.

A year and a half. Walking and running. So busy and happy.

Now everything was about to change again.

Would Z be happy?

She bent to kiss Sophia's tiny fingers, breathing in the fragrance of baby soap.

He'd said he would like more children, and her husband never lied. Wasn't it odd how reassuring that was? She grinned, thinking of all the jokes about "Tell me the truth. Does this dress make my hips look big?"

If Z was asked if a dress made a woman look fat, he'd tell her... politely...that another dress looked better on her. If he didn't like a food, he'd tell Jessica it wasn't his favorite, rather than them getting stuck eating it because he'd lied and told her it was great.

She'd never realized how much tension it created not being sure if a person was being "polite" or not. But Z knew. And she could trust him to tell her the truth, no matter how hard.

God, she loved him. As her husband, her lover, her Dom.

Hearing the beep-beep-beep of the security system as he let himself into the kitchen, she smiled. Finally. Earlier, he'd called to say both he and the car had bad days. He'd run into something sharp and ripped up his arm enough for stitches. And the car windshield had gotten cracked, so it was in the shop, and he had to get a rental.

Poor Z.

As was his way, he came straight to her. He never returned home without giving her a hug and kiss.

In the dim nursery, he was a dark shape, then a warm length pressed against her back. His arms came around her, and he rubbed his cheek on the top of her hair before turning her and kissing her. Long and sweet. "It's good to be home," he murmured.

She put her arms around his neck and got another kiss. "Your commute is getting longer each year. When we look for a new house, we should find one closer to your office."

"That might be wise." After bending to kiss Sophia's forehead, he put an arm around Jessica's waist and drew her out to the living room.

In the brighter light of the room, she could see that his face was drawn tight, the lines beside his mouth and between his brows deep.

She ran her hand over his cheek. "Are you all right?"

"Rough day." His smile seemed forced. "Being home helps."

That had been her goal—to make his home a sanctuary. Because he deserved it.

Admittedly, they both worked hard at their jobs, but he counseled traumatized children as well as combat vets with PTSD. In comparison, her job was relatively stress-free. Well, except for around tax season.

"Did something happen?"

He paused, frowned, and took her hand and kissed her fingers. "An old friend called. He's got cancer, and it doesn't look good."

"Oh, oh Z." She could see the pain in his gray eyes and the frustration. She'd learned that nothing frustrated a Dominant more than being unable to fix. To help. To keep everyone safe and happy.

Especially friends and family.

"I'm sorry. What can I do?"

"Nothing, I'm afraid. He lives in Alaska." Z's lips quirked. "He told me to keep my ass home. He didn't need help and would shoot the first person to show up at his door."

She blinked. "Well, that's definite."

"He's a bit paranoid. Well, more than a bit. But right now, he's up and moving. Says he's not in pain. Later...later might be different."

"All right then." She took his hand. "We'll go up later."

He gave hers a squeeze. "Yes. I'd appreciate that."

Needing to get the haunted look out of his eyes, she turned the subject to Sophia. How their daughter had danced to "Can't

Stop the Feeling," and ended up looking like a squirmy worm. While trying to clap.

Her after-bath, toweled-off dash through the house. Naked.

That description got a grin...because Z had bathed his girl the night before with the same results.

She told him about reading a book. When Jessica had imitated ducks with "Quack, quack, quack," Sophia had bellowed out, "*Whack, whack, whack!*"

The sound of Z's laughter still had the power to send a thrill through Jessica.

Maybe she should wait to tell him the news? Maybe she should give him a drink first. "I need some water. Let me get you a Glenlivet, while I'm there."

Relaxing back on the long couch, Zachary smiled as Jessica handed him a glass of scotch and settled beside him. "Thank you, kitten."

Her hair held the light scent of flowers, and when he kissed her neck, he could smell her fragrance, which was mingled with baby soap. She'd cuddled with Sophia before putting the imp to bed.

Jessica loved to touch. She was like the kitten he called her, sensuous and responsive, a toucher and a snuggler. And full of attitude.

To avoid upsetting her, he'd changed into one of the spare shirts he kept in the car. Seeing the bloody one wouldn't have gone over well with her.

How was she going to take hearing that someone wanted to kill her husband?

He might have a doctorate in psychology, but there was no therapeutic way to dispense that kind of news.

I got a death threat today? No, that'd be a poor way to start.

I enjoyed a police station and ER visit today because someone shot me? Not a chance.

I bought a new car seat on the way home and this is why? Never.

He might be her Dominant in a sexual context, but they had equal footing during daylight hours. Mostly. Which meant he needed to suppress his instinct to protect her. She'd want to know he was in danger and that he'd been hurt. *Shot*. It was her right.

After setting his drink down, he took her hands in his. "Jessica. I think there's something we need to talk about."

She stared at him and scowled. "You know, don't you? All those wicked psychological powers you have, and you looked at me and could just tell."

His thoughts weren't merely derailed, but sent right off a cliff. "I could tell what—"

"It was my breasts that gave it away, right? How big they're getting again? Or...you told me you didn't keep track of my periods, but you did, didn't you?"

Bigger breasts. Periods. A joyous warmth spread through him. "Pregnant? Are we having a baby?"

Her smile could brighten an entire room. A universe.

His universe.

"Yes. A baby. A brother or sister for Sophia." She threw herself into his arms. "Are you happy?"

A baby. "It's the finest present you could ever give me." He pulled her against him, wrapping his arms around his love. And someone new.

There was a spark of life growing inside her.

Awe enfolded him. Along with a heart-shuddering wave of protectiveness. His Jessica was one of the strongest women he knew, but...she was pregnant.

There was no way he could tell her now that someone was trying to kill him, let alone that the man had nearly succeeded.

CHAPTER TWO

The next night, Jessica turned over in their big bed. The Egyptian cotton sateen sheets were cool against her skin... because there was no warm body next to hers. No muscular arm anchored her to the bed. No hand cupped her breast.

Z had disappeared from their bed sometime during the night.

Just like he had last night. *What's going on, Z?*

Jessica slid out of bed and padded through the rooms. All quiet. The Shadowlands BDSM Club on the first two floors of the big stone mansion was closed on weekdays.

The third floor was their family space.

In the nursery, Sophia slept peacefully, her tiny hand curled up beside her face. Jessica's heart melted at the sight...as it had every day for the last year and a half.

But Z wasn't in the nursery.

He wasn't in the living room or his den.

In the kitchen, she noticed the backdoor security light was off.

After grabbing a baby monitor from the kitchen table, she let herself out the door and went down the outside stairs to the patio.

Rain pattered on the palms and tapped on the covered enclosure. In the distance, a barred owl hooted hopefully: *Who cooks for you; who cooks for you all* and received no response. Past the landscaped gardens, the faintest glow of dawn showed.

Leaning against a post, Z was watching the diminishing night. Clad only in loose cotton pants, he was barefoot and barechested. A glass was in his lean hand, but he wasn't drinking.

The bandage over his deltoid was a white square against his tan skin. He hadn't told her exactly what happened. "I got nailed by something sharp," he'd said when they went to bed yesterday. Then he'd diverted her with his far-too-knowledgeable hands and kisses. Celebrating life, he'd called it.

She huffed a laugh. Really, making love with Master Z should be called death-by-orgasm instead.

Hearing her steps on the patio, he turned.

"Couldn't sleep?" she asked.

"Kitten, it's too chilly out here for you. Go on back to bed." His smile didn't reach his eyes.

She hadn't been cold until now.

When he put his arm around her, she snuggled close. "What's going on? You're not sleeping. Are you worried about something? Is it because I'm pregnant?"

Touching her cheek lightly, he shook his head. "No, Jessica, nothing like that. I couldn't be happier about a new baby."

"Then what? Work?"

"I wish." He hesitated as if searching for the right words. "I don't want to frighten you, but there are reports of a man with a rifle prowling around the area."

"Oh my God. Around here?" *How creepy.*

"Close enough," he said grimly.

"That's scary all right." At least their home was safe. When Sophia was born, Simon Demakis, one of Z's friends, had insisted on installing an extensive security system on the house and grounds, as well.

She frowned. "Are you worried about me and Sophia? That's why you can't sleep?"

"Indeed." His arms tightened around her. "If you and Sophia could stay home for a few days until he's caught, you would relieve my mind. The thought of you out on the road makes me uneasy."

She had a home office, and client interactions were mostly online these days. "I can do that."

"Thank you. Also, because of our isolation out here, I've hired a couple of guards to keep an eye on things."

"Isn't that a touch excessive?"

"Not when it comes to your safety, little one. And Sophia." He touched her midriff gently. "And this new spark."

She let out a sigh. There were things that could be negotiated, but when it came to protecting family, Z was as movable as a mountain.

He rested his chin on top of her head, simply holding her. Iron-strong arms, rock-hard body. As long as he was near, she never feared for her safety. But he released her. "Go on back to bed. You're sleeping for two—and Sophia will be up soon."

"But..." Any other time, Z would have escorted her to bed and fucked them both into a good night's sleep. Would have tied her hands to the headboard while he drove her crazy. He might have even gagged her under the pretext she shouldn't wake the baby.

Right now, they probably both needed the comfort of that intimate sharing. She leaned into him, letting her breasts press against his chest.

And heard the monitor squeak. Sophia was awake. Early. Didn't that just figure? "All right."

Tilting her head up, he kissed her, slow and sweet.

As she climbed the stairs, she glanced back.

He was staring out into the rain again.

CHAPTER THREE

The next afternoon, in their home gym, Zachary pushed the bar of weights over his head despite the way his biceps and triceps protested. Exhaustion pulled at his bones. When he rose to reduce the weight on the bench press, his muscles felt as if he was carrying lead weights.

The lack of sleep since Monday was having an effect.

Doggedly, he continued, moving to incline presses, then to military presses.

He still had a couple of counseling appointments and would need to return to the office, but he'd wanted to see Jessica and Sophia.

And, honestly, he'd needed a break in the day. Although he had a gift for communicating with and understanding non-verbal patients, over time, the pain of his patients soaked into him, accumulating in his soul. Being with Jessica lightened that weight.

And the times when he got through to a patient made the burden bearable.

Today, he'd reached a child. Seen her glimpse a bit of light through the wall she'd built around herself. For a moment, she'd stopped rocking, looked at him, and met his gaze. The abuse she'd endured at the hands of her own parents had been horrendous. If they hadn't been behind bars, he'd have killed them himself.

This week? Well, having a stalker made for sleepless nights and stressful days. Between the combat vets he was counseling and the threat to his life, he felt as if he was back in the Army Special Forces. Hypervigilant. Never able to relax.

Corpses, gore, and screams haunted his dreams. Now the lifeless bodies he saw were those of Sophia and his Jessica. *Dammit.*

He turned on the bench, chose a dumbbell, and started on biceps curls.

Although he was trying to keep everything on an even keel, Jessica was worried about him. She had good cause, and he was wrong, in a way, not to tell her everything.

If she were in danger, he'd want to know. Yet she could do nothing about the stalker except be terrified. She still had occasional nightmares from when human traffickers had kidnapped her.

And now she was carrying their baby.

A baby. A new life that they'd created between them. Was there anything more awe-inspiring?

He shook his head. Normally, his protectiveness toward his wife and daughter was, perhaps, somewhat excessive. With Jessica's pregnancy, it had grown out of bounds.

His best move was to deal with the stalker as quickly as possible.

Although the police were looking for leads, he'd gone ahead and hired his friend, Galen Kouros. The ex-FBI agent ran a private investigation company and had a talent for digging out information.

When the security monitor beeped and displayed Galen's car entering the parking lot, Zachary shook his head. *Speak of the devil.*

A minute later, the buzzer on the garden gate sounded. Galen looked at the camera and held up a hand.

Zachary punched in the code to open the gate.

"It looks as if Galen's here, Z." Jessica stood in the door of the gym.

"I'll let him in. Thank you, kitten." After wiping his face with a towel, he bent to give her a quick kiss. "Is Sophia down for her nap?"

"Yes. Hedda just left." Jessica smiled. "Our munchkin is all mine for the rest of the day." Nearing sixty, the nanny stayed with Sophia mornings while Jessica worked in her home office. Jessica had admitted that, even though she loved her job, she also resented every moment the nanny was with Sophia.

"Good enough. In a month or two, we might want to increase Hedda's hours, kitten." His two sons were in their twenties now, but he still remembered how much more work two children were than just one.

At least this time, not being in the service, he'd be around to help.

Jessica pressed a hand to her waist, undoubtedly remembering how big she'd gotten during her previous pregnancy. Trying to keep up with a two-year-old as well as work would be taxing. "We'll see."

His super-wife who thought she could do it all. "I love you."

"You only say that in hopes I'll get derailed from arguing. Nice try." She gave him a quick kiss before heading down the hallway to her office.

Chuckling, he walked across the house, through the kitchen, and opened the door.

Briefcase in hand, Galen was climbing the steps. His Greek heritage showed in the black hair, black eyes, and olive complexion. Having given up the stereotypical FBI image, he was dressed in a white button-down shirt and black jeans.

"Come in." Zachary stepped back. "Can I offer you a drink? Jessica made iced tea, or we have soda, coffee, and water."

"Water would be good." Despite living in Florida for the past few years, Galen hadn't lost his Maine accent.

Zachary handed him a bottle, took one for himself, and motioned toward his den. "Let's talk in there."

Instead of the desk area, he chose the sitting area beneath the wall of books and took a seat on the long couch.

"I saw you're keeping your security system on." Galen cracked open the bottle and took a chair.

"Definitely. No one should be able to get onto the grounds without triggering an alarm. Our windows were already all one-way—because of the club being downstairs. But I have a couple of hired guards patrolling the perimeter as well. I gave them your picture so they wouldn't use you for target practice."

"It's appreciated." Galen grinned. "Have you changed your routine as I suggested?"

"That's difficult. I have patient appointments that have to be kept—my office can't relocate—and there's only one road in front of this house." Just the thought of Jessica on that road made his mouth dry. Zachary cracked open the bottle of water. "What have you discovered?"

"Not enough. The people I've got tailing you report that no one has shown any unusual interest in you. The police say the same."

"I haven't noticed anyone other than your people." Zachary had felt as if he was leading a parade. Galen's men. A bodyguard when he left the house. The two guards on the property.

Jessica had been good about staying home, but her patience wouldn't last, especially since she didn't know about the severity of the threat.

"You're sure the shooter isn't one of your current adult clients?" Galen asked.

"I'm positive." He'd know if a patient wanted to murder him. "Although my clients are often angry with me, it's not a...killing... anger. It's more the reflexive irritation of a badger disturbed in his burrow by someone poking at it with a stick. A defensive reaction, not offensive."

"Maybe you counseled someone badly, and they took it amiss?"

"No, that doesn't fit with the phrasing in the letter I received." Zachary gave Galen a wry smile. "Now, the *'you arrogant asshole'* could come from anyone who's met me."

"Ayuh. Humble, you aren't."

Zachary shot him a look. Maybe he wasn't humble, but the *arrogant* label seemed unwarranted. "The sentence: 'You'll pay for what you did' suggests something more than merely counseling someone."

"You haven't done any business deals where someone would feel taken advantage of?"

"No. Our money is in stocks and bonds."

"I'm sure I'd have heard if you upset anyone at the club." Galen smiled, because his submissive, Sally, collected gossip like a magpie collected shiny objects. "Did you maybe send some poor bastard off to the loony bin?"

"We mental health professionals dislike terms like 'loony bin'." Steepling his fingers, Zachary considered the question. "There have been a few cases where I felt a client endangered the people around him, and I had to take action. All of them thanked me later."

"How about unofficially? Did you ever turn one of your clients in to the police or..." Galen pointed a finger at Zachary. "You're thinking of something. What is it?"

"About a month ago, I attended an event to raise money for veterans. Several active-duty Marines were there, and one... I talked with the man one-on-one for a while." Zachary rubbed his face. "Contrary to popular belief, psychopaths can do well in the military. However, from his behavior—and what his teammates told me privately—he is very unstable, a danger to anyone who crosses him, not just insurgents, but also other military personnel and civilians. Since he was due to deploy soon, I mentioned my concern to his superiors."

"Did anything come of it?"

"I assume he was evaluated by their mental health staff since I received an email from his captain, thanking me for the heads-up." At Galen's frustrated frown, Zachary smiled. "They couldn't tell me more. That's how confidentiality works."

"When it's *my* personal information, I appreciate privacy regulations." Galen scratched his chin. "When I'm investigating someone, I curse the regs up one side and down another."

"I understand. Here's the man's name." Zachary wrote down the name of the Marine as well as the captain and handed the paper to Galen.

"Hewlett Weiss?" Galen stared at the name. "By God, that name right there would be enough to make a man psychotic."

Zachary shook his head. "This is a long shot, Galen. In all reality, I don't know how Weiss would have discovered I said anything."

"Like anywhere, the military is a small world. Secrets get out." Galen rose. "I should have some answers for you later today."

———

After returning to the downtown office for two counseling sessions, Zachary was late getting home. Because Galen had called.

Weiss was the shooter.

Apparently, his superiors had taken Zachary's warning to heart, ordered a psychological evaluation, and the findings kept Weiss from being deployed. Probably permanently. The Marine loved to kill, and hearing he wouldn't return to combat had sent him over the edge. That night, he'd gotten drunk and made threats about the asshole shrink who'd butted into his business. One Zachary Grayson.

The next day, Weiss had left the base. Gone AWOL. Cleaned out his bank account. And disappeared.

So...progress. Now, they just had to find Weiss.

Earlier, one of the guards stationed on the house had called to report he'd scared off someone prowling around outside the fence.

It seemed Zachary had told Jessica the truth about someone with a rifle in the neighborhood.

Zachary sighed and walked into the kitchen.

Blonde hair tied back in a ponytail, Jessica was already making supper, and the aroma of roast beef filled the air. Although a cook visited on Thursdays and left prepared meals to last them a few days, the rest of the time, Jessica preferred to keep their house to themselves. He didn't disagree; he preferred privacy as well. These days, even more than usual.

Between the threats, the guard at his office and on the grounds, and the damn security systems, Zachary felt fenced in. And frustrated.

"Earth to Z." Jessica waved her hand in front of his face. "You disappeared for a minute there."

"I did. Sorry, pet." Pulling her into his arms, he kissed her, breathing in the light floral scent. The fragrance of life. Of beauty.

When he pulled back, she looked up, her forehead creased in thought. She was adorably short and curvy, and far too intelligent for his peace of mind. At least right now. "You don't look...happy."

"I have some rough cases." Simply the truth. He didn't lie, not to her, not to others, yet, he was, dammit. Maybe not in the strictest sense, but he was certainly evading what she wanted to know. "Did Beth reach you? She had a financial question."

"Yes, I got back to her."

Years ago, when Jessica stumbled into his BDSM club, she'd been unfamiliar with the lifestyle. Incredibly innocent, she was also beautifully submissive. Over time, her submission to him had deepened, even as she'd become more assertive with others. In fact, she'd gathered the other Shadowlands Masters' submissives and formed them into a group. Her girl gang, she called it. Anyone in the gang got her canny advice with financial matters.

"Daddeeee." The high squeal came from the living room followed by the thudding of tiny feet. Sophia had heard his voice. He gave Jessica a squeeze and moved to intercept their daughter.

God, she was beautiful. Blonde hair like her mother. His gray eyes. Smart and happy and filled with the wonder of life.

And on her way toward the terrible twos. As a psychologist, he was delighted by her growing independence. As a parent? Knowing everything she was rushing toward was terrifying.

"Sophia." He swung her up in his arms, pushing away the thought of the splintered car seat.

Putting a tiny hand on his cheek, she rubbed her palm over his jaw, giggling at the scratch of stubble.

"How was your day, sweetheart?"

She gave him a serious look. "Goggy."

"Doggy?" Ah, Jessica had mentioned this morning that they planned to visit Rainie who managed a veterinary clinic. The woman was always surrounded by pets needing homes.

"Goggy," Sophia said again. "Me."

No doggy. Totally the last thing he needed, another vulnerable being. "We have a kitty instead." He glanced around, looking for their battered, ginger-striped cat that was normally underfoot during meal preparations. "Where *is* Galahad?"

Sophia's lower lip poked out, and she scowled at the cat door.

A laugh came from Jessica. "Remember the toy Anne gave Sophia last week? When Sophia played it, Galahad fled the building."

"Smart cat." No animal with functioning ears would enjoy that toy. Each button spewed out a different and loud animal sound—meows, barks, moos, baas. The good Mistress Anne was a sadist, but he'd never appreciated the true cruelty in her nature.

Then again, her baby was just getting to a fine age for noisy toys. It would be a shame to miss the opportunity.

"Sophia." Zachary pointed to a soft ball on the floor. "How about we play some ball?" A nice quiet game.

"Baa." Sophia squirmed in his arms to get down so she could show off her latest prowess.

"Daddeeee." Once on the floor, she grabbed his hand and dragged him in the right direction.

There were days she reminded him of Mako. A future Army sergeant. Not that he cared as long as she grew up healthy and happy. Able to stand on her own two feet. Able to give and receive love.

Those were his goals for this precious being.

He glanced back at the kitchen and saw Jessica in the doorway, hand on her belly. Love lit her eyes. For her daughter.

For him.

He would do everything in his power to keep his family safe.

CHAPTER FOUR

As they ate supper, Jessica was grateful for Sophia's babble. At eighteen months, the toddler had decided opinions of the meal offerings. Lacking a whole lot of consonants, her words weren't clear, but her expressions said it all. The tiny chunks of meat loaf proved adequate for Her Highness. Mashed potatoes were amazing—but her displeasure showed when Jessica insisted she use a spoon rather than her fingers. The mastery of utensils wasn't going quickly; however, the sippy cup had only been tipped over once.

Z had actually laughed when she showed her approval of peaches with a "*Nom, nom, nom.*"

Jessica smiled. Her friend Sally had contributed that meaningful addition to Sophia's vocabulary.

But that had been the only time Z laughed.

Heart aching, Jessica gazed at her husband, her Sir, her Master, her love. The silver streaks at his temples had widened. The chiseled lines of his face showed the bones more clearly. He looked tired. Wasn't sleeping.

There was something wrong, more than what he was telling her.

Once the meal was finished, they cleaned up the kitchen together. She did love how Z always did his share in the kitchen.

She was his submissive, not his slave, and over the years, they'd discussed and re-discussed how and where the lines lay in their power exchange. When it came to sex, he was totally the boss...although it was amazing how often a male could view normal activities as a prelude to sexy times. *Sheesh*.

But since they both worked, there was no Dom/sub stuff in the kitchen, and the all-powerful owner of the Shadowlands was okay with that. Maybe because he was a feminist to his core.

She really did love him.

"Thank you for the meal, kitten." Z started the dishwasher, squeezed her shoulder, and walked out to the dining room where he'd left his cell phone. Although they always silenced their phones for meals, he couldn't stay out of touch too long. Not with the kind of patients he had.

After picking up his phone, he checked that Sophia was busy in the living room before turning and winking at Jessica.

Jessica grinned. Their little tyrant had decided phones were toys that should be shared, and she'd throw fits if she didn't get to "talk" on the phone. Unfortunately, for her, she was learning a screaming fit meant she'd be tucked in her room for a quick timeout.

Having spent years running a BDSM club, Master Z wasn't unsettled by a screaming female.

Jessica huffed a laugh. Accountants after the first tax season acquired the same steady nerves. Poor Sophia hadn't found throwing a tantrum to be an effective strategy.

Smiling, Jessica poured apple juice into a sippy cup. Evenings were her favorite part of the day. Time to play roll-the-ball and to see if they could entice Z into joining the game.

On the phone, Z was at the dining room table, making notes on a pad of paper. "Let me check on suitable venues, and you can add the time and location to the funeral announcements. I'm sorry. He was a remarkable man."

As he disconnected the call, the lines beside his mouth and eyes deepened.

Jessica set the juice down and hurried to his side, putting a hand on his shoulder. "What's wrong?"

He laid his hand over hers. "Remember I told you an old friend called to say he had cancer?"

"Yes, I remember. That was only a couple of days ago. You said he was doing all right."

"His lawyer said Mako was driving on a foggy road and went through a railing over a cliff straight into the ocean. He didn't survive." Sorrow had darkened his gray eyes.

"I'm so sorry." She moved closer. An army friend. Although Z had been out of the military for ages, he still had a huge number of military buddies. "Did you serve with him?"

"No. Mako was a Green Beret legend during the Vietnam War and out before I met him."

"Green Beret like you? Special Forces?"

"Mmmhmm. I met him at a military funeral in Los Angeles, maybe twenty-two years ago. He was struggling with PTSD and living in an off-the-grid cabin in Alaska. We talked after the funeral, and I tried to help. Gave him some advice."

Jessica did the calculations in her head. If the sergeant enlisted around eighteen, put in twenty years, and spent ten in retirement, then... "When you met, he'd have been closing in on fifty and you were, maybe, young twenties?"

"Yes. I'm surprised he didn't flatten me."

She could only smile. Even in his twenties, Master Z would have cared for anyone he met. Would have tried to sort them out. "How did he react?"

"He thanked me. Then told me to get my ass out of combat zones and into psychology. He figured a man should dive into the foxhole where he'd be the most use." Z changed his voice to a low rasp. " '*Fuck knows, the army needs shrinks who aren't REMFs.*' "

"REMFs?"

"Vietnam slang—rear-echelon mother-fuckers."

She snorted. "I take it he wanted his shri...uh, counselors to have seen combat. To understand what it was all about."

"After I got out, I took his advice." Z's lips curved slightly. "When a first sergeant gives an order, you obey."

Heart aching at the grief in his voice, Jessica sat down on his lap and put her arms around him. "He lived in Alaska? You must have seen him since, though, if he called you."

"We stayed in touch, yes. After the funeral, on his way out of LA, he took on four orphaned boys to raise. That hadn't been my advice...exactly, but I felt responsible, so I flew up to Alaska now and then to check on how things were going."

That was so like Z. "How did he do with them?"

"They're all good men. Strong, brave, independent. He did well."

And now the man was dead. Sorrow touched her heart.

A notepad lay on the table. Z had written: Saturday. October 7th. Ft. Richardson National Cemetery, Anchorage, Alaska.

Three days from today. "Did you want to attend the funeral?"

Zachary barely heard her. Mako's death felt like the felling of an ancient redwood. The passing of a force of nature.

Only, Zachary had a feeling the old sergeant had gone out exactly the way he'd planned. *Dammit, Mako.*

After a second, he remembered Jessica had asked a question. *Attend the funeral?* He'd promised Mako he'd handle the wake— and check on his sons. He couldn't break that promise, although leaving his family now when someone was targeting him was impossible.

And yet...

If Zachary left, the chances were excellent that Weiss would follow him. Which meant the police would have a good chance of catching him, especially as he tried to board a plane. If Weiss made it to Alaska, then... Well, if needed, Zachary would serve as the bait in a trap. Simon could send some of his highly trained operatives to set it up.

And Mako's sons would be there, four of the most lethal men Zachary had ever met.

Yes, drawing Weiss to Alaska would keep Jessica and Sophia across the continent and out of the field of fire. But, just in case, Zachary would tuck them away somewhere safe and keep them guarded.

"Sorry, pet." He rubbed his cheek against Jessica's. "Yes, I need to go. When Mako called, he asked me to arrange an after-funeral send-off so his boys might remember him as he was. Although they're in their thirties now. Hardly children."

"That's lovely. And no matter how old they are, they'll be hurting. Of course you should go. We can go with you."

He shook his head. "No. Actually, I want you and Sophia to stay with your mother while I'm gone. This place is too isolated for you to be here alone."

"What? Seriously?" She sat up straight and scowled at him.

"Seriously. Either you stay with your mother, or I'll hire guards to stay inside and outside the house and watch over you while I'm gone." Actually, she'd have a guard, no matter what she did.

Her eyes narrowed. "Well, honestly, your Alaska friend isn't the only paranoid one. How about if I leave Sophia with Mom and fly to Anchorage with you."

He cupped her cheek, his heart melting. A few months earlier, he'd encouraged Sophia's grandparents to spend more time with her so he and Jessica could have adult time together. Could eventually enjoy childless weekends. But last month, when he'd suggested three days in Miami, Jessica hadn't been willing to leave the baby for that long.

Now she was willing—because she knew he was hurting.

"Although normally, I'd love to have you with me, this isn't the time. You're pregnant, kitten, and I'm going to be too busy to watch over you." Disliking the need, he hardened his voice. "You absolutely cannot come with me to Alaska."

Although Jessica had been known to...sidestep...his wishes, his sweet little submissive wasn't one to disobey outright. Thank God.

CHAPTER FIVE

On Friday morning, standing in her mother's doorway, Jessica held her daughter's hand as Galen and Vance walked away from the house.

Sophia bounced up and down, waving an exuberant goodbye. "B-b-bye."

Grinning, the men turned and waved back before getting into Vance's car. Delivery of wife, child, and cat completed, they drove away.

I'd better get moving as well. As queasiness rolled through her, she pulled in a slow breath through her nose. With a hand on her still-flat belly, she scolded the imp. *Not now.* As soon as she was on the road, she'd nibble on the crackers in her purse. No time for morning sickness.

Part one of her plan was complete. Part two started now.

This morning at dawn, Z had bid her a loving goodbye before heading off to the airport. An hour later, his two friends had shown up to taxi her, Sophia, and Galahad here to Mom's. Because Z was still all worried about that armed guy in their neighborhood.

If there was one.

Surely she'd have heard something on the news, right?

Or not.

She shook her head. Maybe the police preferred the populace stay ignorant rather than panicking, buying weapons for defense, and accidentally shooting their neighbor. Or worse, their neighbor's dog or cat.

"Those were nice men, weren't they?" her mother asked. "Zachary certainly went out of his way to make sure you got here safely."

Frustration rose inside Jessica. "He goes out of his way to make sure I'm safe everywhere."

As if sharing her irritation with Master Protectiveness, Galahad let out a long yowl from the cat carrier.

"How will he react when you show up in Alaska?"

There was a good chance she might not sit down for a week.

"I'm sure he'll get over it." Her eyes blurred with sudden tears. "He's so sad, Mom. And worried about something, and I don't know what's going on."

When her mom put her arms around her, Jessica absorbed the comfort.

"Knowing you, honey, you'll find out."

Jessica's mouth set. "I will. And whatever it is, I'll help him fix it."

Whether he wants help or not.

Being pregnant didn't make her an invalid, so why was he treating her that way? What was wrong with him?

"Of course, you will."

With a shuddering sigh, Jessica forced a smile and hugged Sophia. "Be good for your Grammie and Aunt Eunice. I know you'll all have a wonderful time."

"We absolutely will." Mom picked up Aunt Eunice's car keys and handed them over. "Drive carefully, sweetheart. And if your husband is upset, I'm going to tell him I knew nothing. Nothing."

Jessica was laughing as she went out the back door, crossed the yard, out the back gate, and into Aunt Eunice's back yard. Because Z might well have tucked a guard in the rental house across the street from Mom's house.

As requested, her aunt's car was parked in front of the house.

As Jessica drove out of town, she realized she was leaving her baby behind...for *days*.

She cried all the way to the airport.

Friday night, Zachary opened his suitcase to hang his clothes up in the hotel room closet. His eyes felt gritty from lack of sleep, his muscles knotted from airplanes and taxis—and worry.

It'd been a long, long day, starting before dawn.

Jessica wasn't happy with him, and even less happy about staying at her mother's house, although the two were close.

Nevertheless, she'd be safe there. The tiny town was a fair distance from Tampa. Galen and Vance had planned to pick her and Sophia—and the cat—up in a vehicle with darkened windows. They would have taken a circuitous route to ensure no one tailed them. At home, the programmed house controls would make it appear as if Jessica was still there.

The guard across the street from Joyce's house would keep an eye on things. Just in case.

Yes, Jessica and Sophia would be safe.

And he missed them already.

Now, all he had to do was oversee Mako's send-off and catch Weiss. Hanging his shirts in the closet, he huffed a laugh. And stay alive. That should probably come first.

As noises came from the adjoining hotel room, Zachary finished unpacking, tapped on the connecting door, and undid the lock.

A minute later, the door opened from the other side.

The man in the doorway was a couple of inches over six feet. Broad shoulders, buzz-cut hair, grim gray-green eyes, and a clean-shaven, strong jaw. Drill sergeant looks—Mako would have approved. "Dr. Grayson."

Zachary stepped back to let him in. "I must admit, you're the first male I've opened a connecting door for."

The man's laugh was sandpaper-rough. "When I play body-guard, having connecting rooms helps." He held out his hand. "DeVries. Simon said to tell you *be careful* and let him know if there's anything else he can do."

Zachary shook the callused hand. "Knowing Simon, that's not all he said."

"Fuck no." DeVries followed him into the living room part of the suite and dropped into a chair. "The rest of the team will fly in tomorrow morning, but if they're not enough, I'm to call for whatever backup we need. Demakis International Security isn't about to lose a client."

"Ah, well, we'll try not to damage DIS's reputation, then." Zachary leaned against the wall.

DeVries's eyes glinted. "And Simon isn't about to lose a friend."

"I'd prefer that outcome myself. Do we have any news about Weiss?"

"Nothing good. He didn't board any plane in Tampa and has no reservations for tomorrow."

A chill struck Z. Had Weiss not followed him to Alaska?

"Or," deVries continued, "he has false ID or didn't fly out of Tampa. Simon's widening the search, but it takes time."

"Understood."

"Once the other three on my team arrive tomorrow, we'll set up a trap. See what happens. Because we're going to assume the bastard is here."

Z nodded. He'd made sure that everyone from work and his

various associations knew he'd be in Anchorage for a funeral. Anyone calling for him would also receive the information.

"You go nowhere without me, and don't set foot outside of this room without me at your side. Agreed?"

"Of course." Zachary motioned to the array of alcoholic beverages along the wet bar and received a negative response. After pouring himself a scotch, he handed deVries a bottled water before sitting. "You don't think Weiss might have stayed in Tampa. For my family?" His worst fear.

"He'll be here. I get the impression he's got tunnel vision when it comes to what he considers an enemy."

Zachary frowned. "I think you have more information than I received."

"Probably. I pulled some strings and talked to his teammates." DeVries's mouth tightened. "They have a strong belief he eliminates people who piss him off. In Iraq, a sergeant kept him from beating up a civilian. The sergeant got killed; a long-range shot came from some half-destroyed buildings. Another teammate he disliked caught a bullet from the rear while in a firefight."

Zachary's gut tightened. "Weiss has crossed the mental boundary from killing for his country to killing for his own ends."

"Looks like, yeah. He's got a short fuse and is obsessed with payback." DeVries fixed Zachary with a hard stare. "You realize there are no guarantees here, Doc. Not if you insist on attending funerals and receptions and shit."

"I'm aware." Zachary gave him a level look. "I also realize that just standing next to me is dangerous. However, I do not want any heroics, like you throwing yourself in front of a bullet for me. Am I clear?"

"Crystal." The even tone said the retired SEAL would do as he wanted.

CHAPTER SIX

S eated in the spacious hotel lobby on Saturday morning, Zachary frowned at his phone. Jessica wasn't answering his calls. Although she'd been frustrated with him when he ordered her to stay in Tampa with Sophia, ignoring his calls wasn't like her.

His frown grew. Perhaps he should have told her about Weiss before leaving.

No. She couldn't help, and if she knew he was in danger, her nightmares would return. And she was carrying their child. His hand tightened on the phone with his frustration. Because he wanted to tell her what was going on. They didn't keep secrets from each other. Not until now.

Guilt was an ugly mass in his gut.

Off to the side, deVries sat at a table, reading a newspaper. Only someone trained to read body language would recognize his readiness for action. The way his hand never moved far from the handgun inside his jacket. The grim set of his mouth indicated either bad headlines...or that he was still furious that the additional agents hadn't arrived in Anchorage. San Francisco was socked in with fog, and their flight had been canceled.

DeVries had excellent skills, but he was only one man.

Zachary glanced around at the people in the lobby. Two were checking out. Several young men and women were arguing about a research project as they headed toward the convention rooms. An elderly couple was getting coffee at the stand. Several people waited for elevators.

No one set off alarms for him.

New movement drew his attention. Through the revolving glass doors, two men entered the lobby. One was almost as big as the mountains on the horizon, the other dark and lean. Mako's sons.

Smiling, Zachary rose and went to meet them in the center of the room. "Bull, Cazador, it's good to see you."

Bull Peleki was a good six four with a heavily muscled body. His golden coloring hinted at his Pacific Islander heritage. His scalp was shaved. A trimmed black goatee was beginning to show some gray.

Now, Zachary really did feel old. Bull had been ten when they first met.

"Grayson. It's been a while." As they shook hands, Bull smiled. "I don't know if I ever thanked you for helping persuade Mako to move to Rescue."

After the grown boys had left home, the cabin's isolation had exacerbated Mako's PTSD and paranoia. Zachary had lent a voice in getting him to move. "I was glad to be of help."

Zachary held out his hand to the other man. "Cazador, how are you?"

Shorter than Zachary by about an inch, Cazador Ramirez had finely sculpted musculature. His Hispanic heritage was obvious from the dark eyes, straight black hair, and brown skin. The most empathetic of the four sons, he'd been a Special Forces medic before obtaining a nurse practitioner license.

"This is a sad way to meet old friends," Cazador said softly.

Over the years, he'd never lost the soft Spanish accent. Hadn't tried, in fact.

"It is." Zachary glanced around. "Are Gabriel and Hawk here?"

"Hawk is undercover overseas for that crappy mercenary outfit he works for. He won't be here." Bull's bass voice held a growl.

"I'm sorry to hear that." Zachary sighed. He'd hoped the two had quit the mercs. Hawk had left the military at the same time as Gabriel, for an unknown reason, had resigned his job as an LA police lieutenant. They'd both been with a private military company for the last couple of years.

"Gabe is here in Anchorage...in the hospital." Cazador's face was grim.

Zachary could feel the frustrated anger coming from both men. "What happened?"

"Some South American assignment turned into a clusterfuck, and Gabe was shot to pieces. At least they were nice enough to transport him back here to recover after his surgery." Cazador shook his head. "It was a long damn flight, and he was still disoriented when we had to tell him about Mako."

Gabriel wouldn't have taken the news well. Of them all, he was the most like Mako.

Bull managed a half-smile. "He's a mess, but you know Gabe. He says he'll be at the funeral, no matter what, even if he has to crawl."

Gabriel was about as obstinate as they came. Zachary shook his head. "He shouldn't—"

"Relax." Cazador grinned. "We're picking him up and will make sure he doesn't overdo."

"That's reassuring. It might help him to be at the funeral." As if anything could assuage grief. "I'm sorry for your loss. Sorry the world has lost a man like Mako."

"Thank you." Cazador's eyes gleamed with tears for a moment.

"The sarge's lawyer said Mako'd asked you to handle the after-funeral reception. Did you need help?"

"My only request is that you come for a while tonight." Zachary motioned to a room opening off the lobby. "As it happens, the hotel has a private lounge."

"An entire lounge? Might be only us there," Bull warned.

There would be far more than that. Zachary still had friends in the Special Ops community, many of whom were alive because of the tough old sergeant.

They would come to honor a Vietnam legend.

And Mako's boys would have some new stories about their father.

Cazador tilted his head, studying Zachary's face. "I don't want to be rude, but you look...can I say...stressed?"

"I picked up a stalker in Tampa, one who might have followed me here."

"Yeah? I know it sucks for you, but I'm in need of something active to do." Bull smiled slowly. "How can we help?"

Zachary hesitated. Mako's sons. Survivalist training, ex-military, deadly. Yet to put them in danger...

"Jesus, spit it out, Grayson," Bull rumbled.

"I do have a bodyguard"—Zachary nodded toward deVries—"but I could use extra eyes watching for someone trying to blow my head off."

"Sure. Do you know what he looks like?" Cazador made a *gimme* gesture.

Zachary pulled his phone out and showed them a photo of Weiss.

"A diversion. Perfect." Bull slapped his brother's shoulder, making him stagger. "I'll swing by my house and pick up my S&W."

"I have my knives." Cazador smiled. "I'll be here with Zachary. Maybe I get the man before you this time, eh, 'mano?"

"In your dreams, bro."

Zachary realized he was smiling. "I am never out of the fight," was one of Mako's favorite sayings. There might be no resemblance in looks, but the first sergeant's attitude had passed one hundred percent to the next generation.

The waiting room of the Anchorage salon was decorated in stark black, gray, and white. Waiting for her Saturday afternoon appointment, Jessica sipped what was supposed to be a calming lemon balm tea.

Come on, calming stuff. Kick in. But whenever she imagined Z's reaction to her arrival at his hotel, any hope of tranquility disappeared.

Maybe she wasn't doing the right thing, but the operative word was *doing*. She wasn't going to leave Z to handle his grief alone. He seemed so controlled all the time people didn't realize how deeply he loved, how much he cared.

Right now, he was hurting and worried, and although he hadn't shared everything as he should have—and she felt like smacking him for that—he needed her. He was her husband...her lover...her friend...her Dom. So many things to her.

He'd always been there for her. This time, she could be the supportive one.

Although that plan had been a dismal failure so far. She took a sip of tea, tasting the subtle lemon, waiting for calmness.

Nope.

What a crappy, horrible trip. Was this karmic justice for disobeying him? He didn't give orders lightly, not Master Z, but when he did, only someone given to insanity ignored them.

She had—and everything had gone wrong.

Honestly, what was wrong with birds these days? She still couldn't believe that some suicidal seagull had flown right into the airplane engine.

The plane had barely taken off. After landing, it'd taken hours to repair. After she missed her connecting flight in Chicago, the airline put her up in a hotel and rebooked her on an early morning flight. She'd arrived in Anchorage too late to make it to the funeral. Which was going on now.

So much for being supportive. *I'm sorry, Z.*

On the way to the hotel, she'd seen herself in the taxi mirror. Talk about death warmed over.

She'd hoped Z would share with her what was wrong. But if he saw her like this, he'd ship her home without a doubt.

Time to armor up with one of a woman's best weapons—her appearance. Which was why she was sitting in this Anchorage salon.

"Jessica?" A strikingly beautiful woman walked out from behind the reception desk, clipboard in hand.

"That's me." Jessica set down her cup and picked up her jacket. A jacket totally inadequate for Alaska. Sheesh, it was cold here.

As Jessica walked up to the reception desk, she wanted to crawl into a hole. The woman was tall, slim, and impeccably dressed. Makeup and hair perfect.

"What are we doing for you this morning?"

"Everything, because..." Jessica blinked back unexpected, unwelcome tears. "Because, well, there are two reasons. First, because of a missed flight, I just spent two days getting to Anchorage."

"Oh, ugh, I hate when that happens. And second?"

"My daughter is eighteen months old now. I've been concentrating on being a mommy for almost two years." Jessica blew out a breath. "I adore my little girl, but I need to feel beautiful and strong right now."

"Oh. My. God." The blonde stopped dead. "It took me *five* years to realize that I'd gotten so caught up in mommydom that I'd lost the rest of who I was. Good for you. Good for *you*."

Even as Jessica's mouth dropped open, the blonde looked her up and down, eyes narrowed. "Leave it to me, sweetie. We are *so* going to fix you up."

Fort Richardson National Cemetery was a peaceful place, Zachary decided as he stood amidst the throng that spilled out from under a canvas canopy. Row upon row of white gravestones filled the snow-dusted lawn all the way to the evergreens around the edges. Along the horizon, the stunning Chugach Mountains lifted into the sky.

Mako would feel at home here, surrounded by his fellow soldiers.

Eyes stinging with tears, Zachary pulled his formal overcoat closer and watched over the proceedings. The number of military in attendance, both retired and active duty, had done Mako proud. The first sergeant had given his country his best; they would do no less for him.

The flag-draped casket had a six-man honor guard lining the sides. At the head, the chaplain was finishing the committal service.

As those seated rose to their feet, the rifle party, a distance away, fired a three-volley salute.

A cold chill ran up Zachary's spine as the rifle fire reminded him of his narrow escape. He glanced at deVries who stood alone, leaving himself a clear field of fire. Catching Zachary's look, the security guard nodded and continued watching for snipers, although it was highly unlikely Weiss could get himself, let alone a weapon, through base security.

Nonetheless, before they'd left the hotel, Zachary had requested a weapon, knowing deVries was the type to have packed extras. The Glock 26 was now in an ankle holster, and the weight of the heavy, but small semi-automatic was oddly reassuring.

The rifle volley complete, the lone bugler straightened. As the mournful sound of "Taps" drifted over the cemetery, Zachary had to swallow hard.

The folded flag that had covered the casket was solemnly presented to Gabriel, Mako's oldest son, who was seated in a chair with a cane leaning against his leg.

After shaking hands with the white-gloved honor guard, all three sons moved to the casket to say farewell to the man who'd been, to all intents and purposes, their father. Mako had pulled them out of an ugly situation in a foster care home and raised them in a cabin with no power and no running water.

After leaving home, they'd all served in the military, and so had the straight posture, situational awareness, and dangerous grace of trained human weapons. Despite their hard faces, grief poured off all three.

As the sons moved away from the casket, they were wiping their eyes. Anyone looking at them could see how deadly they were—but somehow, that harsh old sergeant had also taught them to love.

Mako had been a master of war, but he'd known love was the strongest force in the universe.

———

Blinking hard, Gabriel MacNair moved away from Mako's casket. He couldn't imagine the forceful, uncompromising first sergeant inside a...a damned box. It was just wrong.

Gabe's heart hurt, the ache rivaling the throbbing pain in his hip, the harsh burn in his shoulder. His doctors hadn't wanted him to leave the hospital...as if they had any say in the matter. No fucking pain would keep him from saying goodbye to the man who'd raised him.

Saved him.

"Sit before you fall, *viejo*." Cazador's accent was thick today, as if grief had sent him back to the days when he spoke only Spanish.

Gabe glanced down. *Seriously?* "Where the hell did you get a wheelchair?"

"I asked the hospital for one and put it in the trunk before I got you." Despite the signs of tears, Caz's eyes held laughter. He always enjoyed putting one over on Gabe.

"Sneaky bastard." Gabe's chuckle turned raw...because Mako's greatest gift to them was how he'd turned four orphans into family. Into brothers.

"*Sí.* Now sit."

Gabe did because, Jesus, he hurt. And he wasn't ready to leave. Couldn't bear to leave. Stupid to think the sarge would be lonely or feel abandoned without them here, but...he couldn't leave. Not yet. He cleared the thickness from his throat and looked up at his brother. "There are a lot of people here. Are we doing anything afterward for them?"

He'd lost enough teammates over the years to know that usually a reception or something followed, but drugged up on pain meds and in the hospital, he hadn't helped with the funeral arrangements. A pang ripped through his heart again. Funeral and the sarge—the two words didn't go together.

"Tonight, *sí.* When Mako knew...when he started getting weaker, he called Zachary Grayson with orders on what he wanted done."

Grayson? Gabe forced himself to think. Yeah, right. The man had been one of the few who knew the location of Mako's isolated cabin. Of those, only a handful ever braved the crappy dirt road to get there, but Grayson had visited several times.

"He's there, talking to the chaplain." Caz nodded to the right.

Gabe looked over.

Six feet, fit and lean, military posture, dark tan. Aside from the silvering black hair, the man hadn't changed much over the years.

Noticing Gabe, Grayson excused himself to the chaplain and walked over.

"Gabriel. I'm sorry," he said simply, taking Gabe's hand.

"Yeah, me too. Thank you." Gabe eyed him. "Caz said Mako talked with you before...?"

Before the sarge deliberately drove off a fucking cliff into the fucking ocean. Anger stirred within him. *Why, Sarge?*

"He did." Grayson set his hand on Gabe's shoulder as if he could hear the ugly thoughts. "He'd received the diagnosis quite a while before. They told him he could live a few months longer if he'd undergo chemotherapy. He wasn't interested."

Chemotherapy. IVs and drugs and hospitals, weakness and nausea. The sarge hadn't even wanted people to know where he lived. Would he have been able to tolerate a hospital room, surrounded by strange noises? People he didn't know?

Gabe's anger faded. "Yeah, Mako didn't do hospitals." Despite the pain in his heart, he found a smile as he glanced at Caz. "Remember when he busted his arm and made the four of us set it?"

"Mako didn't like doctors much more than hospitals." Caz grinned. "*Dios*, I was scared. We'd only been with him maybe six months?"

" 'Bout that, yeah."

Grayson frowned. "Six months? You were just children."

"No, sir. We were his team," Caz said. "And his orders were as close to God's commandments as you can get."

"Ah, yes, that I do know. Which is why when the first sergeant ordered me to arrange an Irish wake—a send-off—that's what I did." Grayson met Gabe's gaze. "Mako said, 'Find a place with decent booze where whoever shows up can raise a glass and tell a few stories. Share the stupid shit I did when I was younger.'"

Yeah, that sounded like the sarge. Paranoid as hell yet unafraid of dying. He'd figured death was just the next step in an interesting—although occasionally fucked-up—journey. "Where and when is this taking place?"

"This evening at the hotel where most of us are staying. It caters to business people and has a private bar and lounge. There's decent booze, and the hotel will provide a bartender." Grayson's gaze dropped to Gabe's cane. "It has a fireplace, and the seating is comfortable."

Gabe relaxed. He'd have gone, no matter what, but it would've been a bitch to stand for hours or sit in an uncomfortable folding chair like at some receptions. "Thanks. Guess I better see if I can book a room for tonight."

"Zachary already reserved us rooms, *viejo*." Caz huffed a laugh. "You'll know the hotel—Grizzly Towers. On your old beat, right?"

"I'd forgotten you started your law enforcement career in Anchorage." Grayson smiled faintly. "I'd better get back and make sure everything is set up. I hope we have time to talk more this evening." After a firm nod, he strolled away.

"Good man," Caz noted.

"Yeah." Mako hadn't let many people in, but the ones he did trust were stellar.

After his gaze swept over the grounds, Caz pointed to the car. "We'd better be going, too. Bull's waiting for us."

"I see that." Gabe eyed his brother. "Want to tell me why you two are scoping out the surroundings every few seconds? And why Bull is carrying at a funeral?"

"Ah...later."

All right, maybe a cemetery wasn't a good place to have a talk. "Then let's get going." He put his hands on the wheelchair arms to rise.

Before he could, Caz had stepped behind and started pushing.

"For fuck's sake, I can walk to the damn car." The sarge wasn't the only one who despised being helpless.

"Save your strength."

The cane was a solid weight in his hands. How difficult would a backward whap be? Might teach his little brother some respect. Gabe tightened his grip on the cane and glanced back at his target.

Caz made a tsking sound. "Ah, *viejo*, you realize I never have less than four knives on me?"

"Still? Aren't you supposed to be a fucking healthcare professional?" With an annoyed grunt, Gabe sat back.

Multiple knives trumped a single cane any day of the week.

Moving to the side of the guests, Zachary tried—again—to reach Jessica. She still wasn't answering her phone. This was more than her being absent-minded or angry. His worry ratcheted higher.

Pulling up his contact list, he called Jessica's mother. "Joyce, I'm sorry to bother you, but I'm having trouble reaching Jessica. Did she tell you I was in Alaska for a few days?"

With a scowl, DeVries caught Zachary's attention and motioned for him to head out. The committal shelter had cleared of people, leaving the area too exposed.

Giving him an acquiescing nod, Zachary started toward the waiting limousine.

"Why, yes. I know you're in Alaska," Joyce said. There was a long pause. "Are you saying Jessica isn't with you?"

"With...me?" Ice filled him. Had the stalker taken her? Taken Sophia? "When did you last see her?"

"When she dropped Sophia off yesterday morning. Then she borrowed Eunice's car and drove to the airport. To join you in Alaska."

To join him? "I see." She was coming here? He pulled in a long breath, forcing himself to think.

If she'd taken a flight after his, she'd have arrived quite late last night. Why hadn't she joined him in his hotel room?

On the road, vehicles pulled away, leaving the two limousines parked at the curb.

"Zachary, if she didn't meet you, then where is she?" Joyce's voice was tight with worry.

"She's undoubtedly planning an elaborate surprise for later today, which I've obviously ruined," he said lightly, because it was probably true. Must be true.

"Oh, you're right. That would be like her, wouldn't it? That girl."

"I'll have her call you when I see her." He paused, needing the reassurance of hearing his daughter's voice. "If Sophia is awake, can you hold the phone for her so I can say hello?"

"Of course. She's helping me make sugar cookies."

The little mite was probably covered in batter from head to toes.

"Listen, Sophia, here's your daddy." There was a rustling sound, followed by a more distant, "Go ahead, Zachary."

"Sophia, sweetheart, it's Daddy."

The high squeal of delight made his eyes burn. "Dada. Dada. Coooses."

"Yes, you're making cookies with Grammie. You're a good helper."

A spate of words followed, too many consonants missing to be intelligible, but the enthusiasm was obvious.

He took a guess. "Grammie gave you bites of the cookie batter?"

A rolling infectious giggle indicated he was correct. Thumping sounded over the phone. The spoon, perhaps. "Coooses. Nom, nom, nom."

"Have a bite for me, then." He rubbed his hand over his stinging eyes. "I love you, my daughter. Love you very much."

After another word with Joyce, he put his phone back in his jacket.

DeVries scowled, fell in beside him, and jerked his head toward the cars. "Move faster, Doc."

With a nod, Zachary picked up the pace. Would Jessica be at the hotel? That would be the first place to check.

Seeing them approach, their limousine driver got out of the vehicle to open the back door.

Mako's sons were beside the remaining limo. Only the funeral staff and one soldier remained behind.

"Shooter!" Bull roared.

Shoving deVries away to the right, Zachary dove to the left.

A rifle cracked. Pain burned across his side.

From the sound, the shooter was outside the base boundary, somewhere in the forested area. Moving fast with deVries beside him, Zachary made it into the cover of the limo.

"Stay down." DeVries snapped out. He had his pistol aimed... and held fire.

The distance was too great. Zachary didn't bother to pull out the Glock in his ankle holster. Instead, he checked the people at risk.

The driver was crouched to his left.

All ex-military, Mako's three sons had taken cover behind their limo along with their driver.

Beside Zachary, deVries rose. "Fuck it all. He's gone. I couldn't—"

"No, you've only got a pistol. I'd guess Weiss used a sniper rifle." Returning fire with anything less accurate would not only be useless, but might hit civilians.

"Who was the shooter aiming at?" The rumbling question came from Gabe. His tanned face was gray with pain.

"I'm the target." With a grimace, Zachary pressed his hand to the painful wound on his side.

"Damn-it-all, you're hit." DeVries pulled off Zachary's overcoat.

After unbuttoning his shirt, Zachary glanced down. A long furrow ran along the outside of his lower ribs. He'd been lucky. A couple of inches over, and the bullet would have hit his liver. "It's not that bad."

"I'll slap a bandage over it once we're gone." Scowling, deVries glanced at the others. "Bug-out time, in case he comes back for another shot."

Zachary looked at Gabriel. His brothers had obviously not let him in on the information. "I'll explain back at the hotel."

"We have a meeting with Mako's lawyer now." Cazador rose, sliding a knife back into an arm sheath. "But it can be postponed."

Even Gabriel, hurting and fresh from the hospital, looked as if he'd happily strap on a pistol and jump into the fight.

"Thank you, no. The hotel is safe enough." Worry ripped through him. Weiss was here. Where was Jessica?

"At least you know your stalker made it to Alaska," Bull said cheerfully. "And apparently has your schedule."

"The good news just keeps coming." With a sour expression, deVries motioned Zachary into the backseat and glanced at the driver. "Get us out of here."

"Yes, sir."

By the time the limousine reached the hotel, deVries had taped up Zachary's wound and was on the phone to his boss.

"He did what?" he said into the cell, then glanced at Zachary. "Weiss must've heard on Thursday about your plans. He booked a private plane to Atlanta and flew out from there. Got here early Friday morning."

"I see." No wonder the Tampa police hadn't found him at the airport. "He moved fast."

"Too fucking fast." Simon's security guard was seething with frustrated rage. If deVries got a clear shot, Weiss wouldn't survive the encounter.

Zachary put a few extra sterile pads and tape into his pants pockets for later, then handed the first aid kit to the driver. "Add the supplies I used to the bill, please."

"Got it." The driver brought the limo to a halt in front of the hotel doors.

When Zachary reached for the door handle, deVries shot him a look that made him sit back.

As deVries jumped out, Zachary tried to find a modicum of patience. Allowing others to assume the risks for him was intolerable. Even worse, the stalker was a danger to everyone in the area. Speaking of which...

Zachary handed the limo driver several large bills as a bonus. "Thank you for your driving. I'm sorry for the scare."

"No problem." The driver grinned. "Being shot at is a great adrenaline jolt. I'll be able to skip my afternoon coffee. You be careful out there, Mr. Grayson."

"Thank you, I will."

DeVries opened the back door. "Let's get inside."

After gathering his overcoat, Zachary stepped out.

Once in the lobby, deVries let out a long breath. When they'd checked in, the bodyguard had evaluated the room and decided it was fairly safe. No windows for snipers to utilize, too many people, too much movement. Poor lines of retreat.

That was assuming Weiss was rational, though.

And Jessica was here. Maybe. Had she made it to her plane? To Anchorage? Anxiety was a hard knot in his belly.

First step, he needed to know if she'd reached the hotel. Before leaving, he'd given her the hotel name in case she had any problem reaching his cell. He walked to the concierge desk.

Ivan smiled. "It's good to see you today, sir. What can I help you with?"

"Could you check if my wife arrived last night? Jessica Grayson. Perhaps she was so late she didn't want to disturb me?"

"Of course. Give me a moment." Ivan turned to his computer,

tapping quickly. "Ah, no. I have no one by that name inquiring for you or checking in."

She hadn't arrived. Fear swept through him, and he forced it down. "She isn't answering her cell, and I'm worried."

He still hoped the reason she wasn't answering had nothing to do with Weiss and everything to do with the little submissive's motivations. As long as Jessica could avoid speaking to her Dom, she could dodge his awkward questions.

His mouth tightened. Once he found her, they'd be having a conversation, one uncomfortable for both of them.

He should have told her about Weiss. That was *his* mistake.

They would definitely talk about her disregarding his orders.

He managed a smile for the concierge. "If she does arrive, can you call me?"

"Of course, sir. Immediately."

"Thank you." He caught deVries's gaze and motioned toward the elevators. "Let's go. I need to start making phone calls." Galen could check the airlines and...

"And clean that wound and change. Good thing you're wearing black, or you'd have questions to answer." DeVries slowed, his gaze on the front door. "Ah...Simon showed me your file."

Not a surprise. The owner of Demakis International Security kept files on everyone. "And?"

"And isn't that your woman?"

Pulling a small suitcase, Jessica was crossing the lobby toward the elevators. In a green jacket that matched her eyes, and with her blonde hair bouncing, she drew all eyes with her vibrant energy.

Fear was a cold blade inside him as he remembered the crack of the rifle at the cemetery. He had pushed deVries away to get him out of the line of fire. It could have been Jessica beside him. Her buoyant beauty could so easily have been wiped out today.

He raised his voice. "Jessica."

She spun, saw him, and her eyes lit. Then her pleasure dimmed with uncertainty.

His anger flickered to life, mingling with fear.

"Uh, hey. Sir. I thought I'd join you. Be here as your support." She wet her lips. Lips that would always soften under his.

Lips that would be cold and stiff if she was dead.

"I told you *no*." The fear inside him made him less than tactful. And anger made him insensitive. "I didn't want you here with me."

She moved closer. "You might not want me, but you do need me."

"No."

Her flinch made him hurt—almost as much as the bullet wound in his side hurt.

She could die here.

He pulled in a breath. "I realize you simply wanted to help, but this isn't... You can't be here."

"But why?"

Dammit. "Jessica, I love you, but I need you to go home. We'll discuss what's happening when I return."

"What's happening?" Her stubborn little chin lifted. "I *knew* there's something wrong, more than your friend's passing. What is really going on?"

Normally, he loved her persistence and determination. This time, her intransigence was like rubbing salt into an oozing scrape. "What is going on is that you're going home."

Jessica stood paralyzed as her husband turned into her Dom, right there in the hotel lobby.

His eyes turned steely; his deep voice sharpened, and the power he usually kept subdued shook her. "I'll have someone take you to the airport."

He glanced to the right, and a man standing nearby shook his head. "Nope. Taxi service isn't in my job description."

Z growled under his breath, took a slow breath, and she could see him work to conquer his anger. "It wouldn't be safe to put you into a taxi."

"Safe?" The words inside struggled to come forth. "Z, please." She took a step forward and put her hands on his waist, hoping against hope he'd wrap his arms around her.

He flinched instead and stepped back. Away from her. "I want you to wait right here. Then we'll go up to the suite."

As her eyes filled with betraying tears, she nodded.

Struggling for control, Zachary walked a few steps away from her. He was far too angry, and even worse, afraid. A person couldn't have a rational discussion from a place of fear. He wouldn't hear what she said, wouldn't consider his own words.

Letting out a slow breath, he glanced at deVries. "How do I keep her safe?"

Ignoring the question, deVries scowled. "That was a real goatfuck, Grayson."

"Indeed. However, my relationship isn't what I wanted your opinion on." When deVries stayed silent, Zachary continued, "How soon will the other operators be here?"

"Fucking airport. Not till late tonight." The man's brows drew together as he glanced at Jessica.

Zachary found a trace of amusement. Simon's cold-blooded sadist was worried about her. "I'm taking her up to my room to talk."

"You need to tell her what's going on, Doc."

"I know." He rubbed his face. "Actually, I'd planned to lead with that, but I let fear control my tongue."

"No shit. You know, it's reassuring that even big shot psychologists fuck things up now and then."

Zachary gave him a wry look. "You're not helping."

"Couples counseling isn't in my job description."

Trying not to cry, trying to think about anything except Z's anger, Jessica walked down the corridor beside him. Silently.

As Z unlocked the hotel room, the man who'd trailed behind them waited.

Z nodded to him. "I'll be here. Why don't you take a break?"

The man hesitated. "If I have your word you'll call before you open the door again, Doc."

"You have it."

Jessica stared after him. "Who is that man? Is he guarding you? What's going on?"

"Hold on, pet. We're going to talk. Both of us." After tossing his ripped, black overcoat onto the desk, Z locked the door and rolled her suitcase into the bedroom.

Jessica stared after him. She wasn't ready to talk...not just yet. If he yelled at her, she really would burst into tears. "I need to use the bathroom."

Before he could speak, she set her purse and the salon bag on the desk, hurried into the bathroom, and closed the door. Locked the door.

Dropping onto the toilet seat, she sniffled like a wuss. Her tears were partly due to hurt feelings. Because Z had been so...*cold*. He hadn't been happy to see her at all. Yes, he'd just come back from a funeral, but he hadn't wanted to hold her, to take comfort from her. Instead, he'd been furious.

She'd wanted to help him, but he couldn't see past the fact she'd disobeyed him.

Accepting that the Master Z part of him would undoubtedly punish her for her defiance, she'd thought the husband part would welcome her support while he was mourning his friend.

Apparently not.

Needing air, she opened the tiny bathroom window. Decks on the ground floor overlooked a forested creek that curved like a green snake through Anchorage. Past the city were white-topped, jagged mountains under a leaden sky. Spectacular, yes, but there were no palm trees, no pools or tropical flowers, no warm sun. Only cold, gray clouds.

Feeling another tear roll down her cheek, she growled under her breath. The other reason for her tears was sheer frustrated *anger*.

Why was he being so stubborn? He did need her. And he kept shutting her out instead.

Well, he said they'd talk. *Fine*. He'd get an earful.

Heading for the door, she glanced in the mirror and winced. Red eyes, running mascara. That wouldn't do. No need to start at a disadvantage. She turned on the faucet, held her hand under the frigid water, and blinked in surprise.

Pink-red liquid was running down the drain. What in the world? She turned her hand over. Something red had smeared her wrist and palm, and she must have been so preoccupied with Z's reaction she hadn't noticed it before.

Was that *blood*?

She glanced down. No, she hadn't hurt herself.

There hadn't been blood on her hands at the salon. Or in the taxi, for that matter. She'd have noticed when she paid the driver. She'd have noticed if she bumped into a bloody person.

What if she'd tried to hug one?

A cold chill slid through her.

Z's shirt had been damp.

It hadn't rained today.

And when she'd gripped his waist, he'd winced and stepped back. Even if he hadn't wanted her hug, he wouldn't have winced.

Blood wouldn't show on his black attire.

He was injured.

CHAPTER SEVEN

Having mastered his anger, Zachary stood at the living room window, looking out at the gray skies.

The door to the bathroom flew open. Face flushed, hair loose around her shoulders, Jessica stomped out.

She was glaring. At him. "You."

He lifted an eyebrow.

She held her hand out. When he tried to take it, she stepped back and made an outraged noise low in her throat. "You are *bleeding*."

Blood streaked her hand. Ah, right. The gunshot wound.

He tilted his head. "I was, yes. That's part of what I'd like to discuss."

The color drained from her face, making her green eyes stand out. "Are you all right? Are you still bleeding? Did someone hurt you?"

Just like that, her temper had vanished, and all her concern was for him. Was it any wonder he loved her?

"Is that why you have that man following you? Are you in trouble?" She grabbed his jacket front, emphasizing her questions with small tugs.

If he started bleeding again, they'd both be unhappy. "Easy, kitten." He set his hands over hers, quieting her.

Her gaze dropped to his side. "Tell me. Please."

Putting more fear into those eyes was the last thing he wanted to do. He hesitated.

When she pulled in a hurt breath, he wanted to curse himself. The Dom who'd promised to protect her at all costs was the one who was harming her.

"I seem to have picked up a stalker. He took a shot at me at the funeral."

"A stalker?" Her voice sharpened. "And he *shot* you?"

"It's just a graze."

"Show me." Her growled "show me" didn't sound meek in the least.

A laugh tickled his throat. She'd sounded like this when they first started seeing each other. When he'd discovered the strength at the heart of this submissive.

Zachary pulled off the bloody jacket and his shirt. The white gauze deVries had taped over his right ribs was still in place.

Jessica stared at the blood streaking his skin. "Your *graze* bled a lot." Her voice shook.

"I know it's a cliché, but it looks worse than it is." He touched her cheek. "The bullet made a shallow furrow through skin and muscle, nothing more."

As her gaze lifted, her eyes narrowed. She pointed to his right upper arm. The rip through his deltoid was still scabbed. "Was that from a bullet, too?"

"Yes."

Her color deepened as her quite obvious fury began to escalate.

He glanced at the loveseat. "Let me sponge off first, then I'll tell you everything."

After a second, she nodded.

When he came out of the bathroom, she handed him one of his black shirts.

"Thank you, kitten." After putting it on, he wrapped his arms around her.

Rather than burrowing closer, she was stiff in his arms. Angry and hurt. Remorse ripped through him. He'd messed this up badly from the start. "I'm sorry."

"Sorry for getting a stalker? For getting shot?"

"Sorry I didn't tell you everything from the start."

She pulled back. "Uh-huh. About that." Her voice rose. "Why *didn't* you tell me?"

Not giving him a chance to answer, she jerked away from him and paced across the room. Kicked the desk chair. Turned back around. "Well? *Well?*"

"I was going to, but..."

"But. Right. There's always a but. You're just like my clients." She kicked the chair again, this time hard enough to send it barreling into the wall. "I planned to keep the receipts, but I got drunk. I would've made that estimated tax payment, but I got a divorce that month. Or laid. Or something. I would've told my wife that someone wanted to kill me, but it just kind of *slipped my mind.*"

Z couldn't blame her. He'd be furious if he discovered she was in danger and didn't tell him. So, he settled onto the loveseat to wait her out as she let off some of her anger.

Was it appalling that he found her outraged ranting adorable?

When the chair hit the wall hard enough to leave a dent, he rose and gripped her shoulders firmly. "Enough, pet."

After eyeing him wrathfully, she let him pull her down beside him on the loveseat.

He took her hands, holding them trapped in his. "I started to explain everything that first day, but that was the night you told me you were pregnant." As the wonder of her announcement swept through him, he shook his head. "I couldn't ruin that moment."

"Oh." Gaze dropping, she stared at the rug.

Finally, she looked up. "I guess I can see how you might have waited. But only until the next day."

"Quite honestly, I'd thought the police would catch him quickly."

"That's why you told me there was an armed man in the neighborhood."

"It is." He sighed. "I didn't want you to worry about me."

"You had someone shooting at you." Her voice was stilted. Disbelieving. "And you didn't want me to *worry*? Are you crazy? Or simply too dumb for words? I can't believe—"

He tightened his grip on her hands to keep her from rising.

"We are partners. Or so I *thought*. You didn't see fit to tell me you were in trouble? Or that Sophia could be in danger, too?" She jumped to her feet. Paced. Kicked the chair again—this time in his direction.

He blocked it with a foot and waited out the new deluge until she sputtered to a stop.

Until she sat down beside him again. "Why, Z? Explain it so I can understand and not kill you and stuff your body under the bed and leave it rotting there for a maid to find." She glanced at the bedroom door. "That would be mean to do to a maid."

Not him, though, hmm?

Yet the fact she didn't hide her anger pleased him. Now, somehow, he had to fix the damage he'd done.

"I thought I had good reasons, but, I can see they weren't good enough."

"What reasons?"

"Because you still have nightmares from your kidnapping. Even the incident at Anne's house brought them back. In addition, we have a child at a demanding age, and you still work. You're pregnant. The last thing you needed was more stress."

"I'm not fragile," she stated through gritted teeth. "If you'd told me, at least I'd have been worrying about the *right* things."

She sucked in a breath and held up a hand to keep him from speaking. "More than that, we're partners, not just Dom/sub. You don't keep secrets from your partner, Z...even if you do want to protect her from all the things that go bump in the night."

Z was listening with that complete focus that said he'd put everything aside to concentrate on her. Her words. Her body language. As if nothing else mattered in the world except her. And a tiny bit of her anger faded.

"You're right. I made a bad decision. Lying by omission was wrong. *I* was wrong. I'm sorry, Jessica, and I apologize"

Her anger diminished further when she saw honest regret in his gray eyes. He really was sorry.

"I can't help wanting to protect you from anything and everything that might hurt you." His deep voice softened. "You gave me a daughter. Watching you two together... Sometimes I'm not sure I can hold all that love. I love you very, very much, Jessica."

"That's not playing fair," she muttered as her heart melted.

When tears spilled from her eyes, he cupped her face and used his thumbs to wipe the wetness from her cheeks.

"You should have told me. About being shot." Her anger rose again. "I'm going to be mad at you for a while."

"Fair enough," he said equably. "As long as I get the same privilege."

"What do you mean?"

"If you get to stay angry at me after I admit I was wrong and apologize, I get to do the same with you when you make a mistake."

Oh...*damn*. She scowled. Because she loved how Master Z's anger didn't linger after she'd apologized.

Or after she'd been punished.

"You should be punished," she grumbled.

"You're right."

She froze. He'd insisted she punish him once and made her hit him with a flogger until his skin welted. The memory was horrible. Hurting him was intolerable. "No. I won't—I can't ever hit you again."

He studied her face, and amusement lit his eyes. "All right, I won't make you beat on your Dom." He pulled her into his arms again, against his broad chest, and like a flood, contentment filled her, messing with her anger. "What can I do to make this right for you?"

Wasn't that just like him? She'd met Doms who never admitted they were wrong, somehow thinking that being in charge meant they never made mistakes. But Z never failed to take responsibility for what he did, never failed to apologize and try to make things right.

God, she loved him so much.

And he was waiting with that unlimited patience of his for her to come up with an answer.

"Let me think about that." She was tempted to come up with something mean, but—she sighed—he wouldn't do that to her.

"All right." He smiled slightly. "Now, about you coming here—"

Inside her purse, her phone rang.

Was something wrong with Sophia? Jessica hurried across the room to her cell and checked the display. "Mom? Is Sophia all right?"

"Mamamamama."

"Sophia." Smiling, Jessica sank down into the closest chair. The longing to be home with her baby was an ache in her heart.

Her mother came on the line. "Are you in Alaska? Zachary called, and I was worried. Are you with him now? Was he surprised?"

"I'm fine. Yes, I'm with him, and uh, I'd say he was surprised." Jessica bit her lip as she glanced over at him.

Z gave a deep laugh.

As her mother continued, Jessica relaxed, loving the report of Sophia's brilliance and charm. Of how many new words she'd learned. Of how she had everyone wrapped around her little finger.

"She tells your Aunt Eunice what to do, and my sister simply does it." Mom's voice was loud enough that Z could hear.

His grin flashed.

Jessica grinned back. There was no denying their daughter had serious management skills. "Yes, Mom. That's right." As she talked, she watched her Dom.

Shirt still unbuttoned, he prowled around the room.

Really, should any man be allowed to look that hot? The solid wall of his chest tapered to a hard-packed abdomen. His black hair was mussed. The angular line of his jaw was shadowed by a day's growth of beard.

With a quizzical frown, he looked in the bag from the salon, which was filled with high-end hair and body products. He opened one bottle and sniffed. When an eyebrow went up and he smiled, she gave a happy, silent sigh.

"And don't forget to watch out for bears," her mother warned. "They have grizzlies there, you know."

It was a two-legged predator with a gun she worried about.

Or maybe the one stalking around her room right now. "Yes, Mom, I'll watch out for bears. I'll let you know when we'll be home. Love you, too. Bye."

Leaning on the desk, Z folded his arms across his chest. The shirt gaped open enough she could see the gauze pad on his side. There was an awful lot of blood staining the white.

She rose. "I need to change that dressing."

"I'll do it. It's nothing you need to see."

Still protecting her. From bad news, crazy stalkers, and ugly wounds. She set her jaw. "I've figured out your punishment, Master Z, and it's in three parts."

"Three parts?" His lips twitched as if he suppressed a smile. "Isn't that excessive?"

"No. You lied—okay, not exactly lied, but evaded the truth—multiple times over multiple days. Right?"

"Indeed." His head tilted. "Go on."

"First part. I'm okay with being shielded physically, but no more trying to protect me emotionally by concealing the truth. That isn't what I need—and isn't what I want for our relationship."

"That's an odd punishment."

"But it's the part you'll probably find the hardest to fulfill." It would go against every protective instinct in his Dominant soul.

His brows drew together, and he nodded. "All right." His gaze met hers. "I have missed sharing everything with you, to be honest."

Her heart melted like ice cream in the sun. Then she shored up her resolve. He wasn't off the hook. Uh-uh.

She paced across the room and drew his shirt apart. "Second part. Actually, though, this is part of the first and not shielding me from emotional stress."

He waited.

"I'm going to change your dressing and do the wound care from now on."

She saw his objections rise and how he bit them back. He nodded.

So she motioned to the bathroom.

"So stubborn." Rummaging in his pants pockets, he pulled out packets of sterile gauze dressings and tape. "Here you go."

"Thank you." As she pulled off the dressing, she saw he hadn't lied to her. The wound was a clean groove, although the sight of the bloody gash in his smooth tanned skin made her want to cry.

She couldn't. Not if she wanted to convince him how strong she was. The wound had stopped bleeding. It was going to be all right. Concentrating fiercely, she washed the gouge and used a new gauze pad and tape to cover it again. "Done."

"Thank you," he said gravely before kissing her lightly. "I'll let you know when it needs to be changed again."

She let out the breath she'd been holding and let him guide her back into the living room.

"You said three parts?" he prompted.

Right. Three. "Third. After that crazy man is arrested, I want a vacation. Just you and me for a couple of days." Because she missed being able to cuddle and talk without listening for a baby monitor. Missed making love without worrying about being interrupted.

If he still wanted to make love to her after she got all angry and demanding.

His eyes narrowed. "What was that thought, right there?"

When she looked away, his fingers closed on her chin and forced her to meet his intent gaze. "Jessica."

"Can I hope you're not so mad that you don't want to make love?"

"Ah." His lips curved in a dangerous smile. "It's a rare moment that I don't want to make love to you. However, I'd be delighted to give you some reassurance."

After taking her lips in a long, warm kiss, he set her back from him. Regarded her slowly. His voice deepened. Darkened. "Strip for me, little one."

A shiver ran through her. When Z turned into Master Z, he had the power to rock her world.

Under his steady, authoritative gaze, she removed her clothing until she stood naked in the center of the room.

"Very nice." With a faint smile, he strolled around her. Inspecting her as a Master would. His hand trailed over her wide hips...and she could feel his appreciation of the beautiful curviness. When he cupped one breast, she could see his pleasure in the heavy lushness. How he enjoyed teasing her nipples to pebbled peaks.

With a ruthless hand, he tilted her head up and took her mouth, his lips firm, kissing her deeply until the floor beneath her shook.

"Stay there." He disappeared into the bedroom and reappeared with the quilt from the bed. After spreading it out on the floor, he set the salon bag beside it.

"Sit there." He pointed to the quilt.

She settled cross-legged in the center.

After stripping, he sat behind her, so close his hard erection pressed against her buttocks. For a moment, far too short a time, he reached around her and played with her breasts, cupping and teasing them.

She felt the haze of arousal settle around her.

He chuckled. "Sorry, kitten, that was just for my own enjoyment. Before I started."

"Started?"

"You're all tensed up." After squirting lotion into his palms, he began to massage her shoulders. Her neck. Her arms. His hands were strong and warm.

As her body loosened up, she realized how stiff she'd been. Not surprising, what with plane flights, waiting rooms, and facing down an annoyed Master.

His fingers hit a knot, dug in painfully, and then all the muscles around it relaxed and warmth flooded that area. "Oooh."

Z's low chuckle filled her ears.

As the air filled with the scent of citrusy vanilla, he murmured, "Mmm. I like this fragrance on you."

The minute she'd sniffed it in the salon, she knew it would appeal to him.

When his hands moved away from her back, the temperature in the room rose. His warm, slightly callused palms slid silkily over her breasts to tease her nipples back to hard points.

Low in her body, a molten pool began to form.

Her breasts were tight and achingly swollen when his stroking moved down to her stomach.

When her head cleared enough that she could move, she turned to kneel, facing him. After getting her own squirt of lotion, she ran her hands over his hard muscled arms.

Looking up, she caught her breath. His gray eyes were the color of steel, filled with a devastating confidence...and heat.

Desire simmered in her bloodstream. Slowly, she traced the divide in his biceps and triceps, avoiding the healing wound on his deltoid. Her fingertips moved down the contoured line between his pectorals, each ridge of his abdominal muscles.

Smiling slightly, he rose to his feet and gave her a look. *Proceed.*

Still on her knees, she leaned forward to kiss the hollow at the angle of his hip and groin. And then she closed her mouth over him.

She heard his low inhalation. He let her enjoy herself for far too brief a time, then gripped her hair. Taking control from her. "Hands behind your back."

Her whine was an audible protest.

The sound of his deep masculine laugh filled her with need.

He was thick and hot as he moved in and out. As her tongue traced the veins, the rougher dent on the underside.

Her head controlled; her hands behind her back; submission and desire. Her body seemed to be melting into the floor.

"There, now, that's enough, kitten."

Pulling himself out of her warm mouth, Zachary settled in front of her on one knee. Because he needed to touch her.

Looking at her, he smiled. Her lips were swollen, her cheeks flushed with arousal. Her breathing was faster.

After taking more lotion, he ran his hands over her, simply

enjoying all those lush curves. He paused. Her skin was incredibly soft. More slowly, he stroked his palms over her back, her ass, her legs. Silky smooth. Someone had utilized the salon's services. "Mmm. Very nice, kitten."

She smiled at him, delighted he was pleased.

After a quick kiss, Zachary cupped her breasts to savor the succulent weight. Her pale pink nipples tightened into hard buds.

When she'd been breastfeeding Sophia, her breasts were heavier, the areolas darker and larger. After weaning, her size had slowly changed back. Now, the nipples were lighter and smaller again. Her breasts had grown a bit softer with a slight sag, which she'd complained about adorably.

Soon they'd grow again for the new babe.

He couldn't imagine any size or shape where he wouldn't want to have his hands on her.

"Stand up and spread your legs," he said softly.

She did.

He watched the color rise from her upper chest into her face as he curved his hands around her hips and used his thumbs to open her labia, exposing the clit. A tremor ran through her as he leaned forward, licked the pink nub—and held her in place.

"Z..."

Ah, she knew better. He nipped an outer fold in reprimand, receiving a more pleasing, "Master!" before enjoying himself a little longer.

In fact, he didn't stop until her clit was swollen and hard...and her knees started to buckle.

Rising, he turned her toward the door. "On the bed, on your back. Legs open, hands over your head."

Her eyes were wide.

Yes, it had been a while since they played in the way they both enjoyed.

Since a delay would only increase her anxious anticipation, he went into the bathroom and took the time to shave off the day's worth of beard-growth. Although he often enjoyed being territorial and marking her with beard burn, they still had to make an appearance at the memorial tonight.

He'd settle for leaving his handprints on her ass instead.

A glance at the gauze dressing on his side showed it was still dry. The wound was a dull ache—nothing that would slow him down. Good enough.

When he walked into the bedroom, the lights had been dimmed, and a beautifully naked blonde lay stretched out on his bed. Fingers laced together, her arms formed a circle above her head. Her lips and cheeks held the glowing flush of excitement. Her nipples were tightly pebbled, the tips a darker pink.

Obediently, she'd parted her legs, exposing a perfectly bare pussy that glistened with her arousal. Yes, she'd been thinking of what would happen as she waited.

"You really are beautiful."

Her eyes lit. In spite of how often he told her, she always looked surprised.

As he walked to the bed, her gaze dropped to his rigid erection. Amusement tilted his lips. She wasn't the only one who was impatient for what was to come.

But he'd make them both wait while he dealt with one unresolved matter. Because he had a cruel streak at times.

Stretching out on his left side, he propped himself up on his elbow while angling his forearm so he could set a hand over her laced fingers and pin her in place.

Her eyes widened as she tested his grip and realized she was trapped.

Was there any Dom in the world who didn't enjoy the first quivering response of a submissive?

Bending down, he kissed her, feeling her lips soften and open to him. Everything, body and soul, lay open to him.

Z's kiss was slow and thorough, and Jessica realized his hand was cupping her breast.

When he pinched her nipple, rolling the peak between his fingers, she wanted—needed—to move, but his other hand kept her arms trapped over her head.

Submission. Her body was on an elevator, sinking downward, all the way to subterranean levels.

Still holding her hands down, he kissed her neck, her collarbone, and bent to suck on each nipple in turn. His free hand stroked over her lower belly and between her legs, sensitizing her clit, her entrance.

She was slick with arousal...and squirming with need.

When he lifted his head, her wet nipples puckered in the cool air of the room. His eyes were thoughtful as he regarded her silently.

"What?" The question almost burst out of her.

"I almost forgot. You deliberately came here, ignoring my orders that you stay home with Sophia."

"You're going to discipline me because I made a decision based on the incomplete information you gave me rather than all the facts? Seriously?" Her head might explode.

"Little one, if I'd told you everything, would you have obeyed me then?"

Her mouth opened. Closed. Because...hearing he was in danger would have only strengthened her resolve to try to help. As long as her daughter was safe, she would have defied him and come here.

And Master Z wouldn't let her disobedience go unpunished.

"I'm screwed, aren't I?" she said glumly.

"You will be, pet. You'll also be spanked."

"I think it's just wrong to beat on the mother of your child."

"Do you?" he asked thoughtfully. Releasing her hands, he pulled them down to her sides as he sat up.

When he didn't yank her across his knees, she had a moment of hope. Was she actually going to win an argument? A D/s argument?

Picking up the oversized pillow at the head of the bed, he set it on her pelvis, and rolled her on top of it. Her face lay against the mattress. Folding her arms across her low back, he secured them with one hand.

The pillow had raised her butt in the air. Oh, God, she *so* hadn't won.

"Who better to beat on than the mother of my child?" He rubbed her bottom and began.

After five light swats, a warm sting bloomed over her buttocks.

"Spread your legs, little one."

A flush of humiliation warmed her face. How many years would she have to be married and submissive before she'd lose all her modesty? It sure hadn't left her yet.

His voice grew softer. "Now."

With a protesting moan, she opened her legs.

His fingers slid over her wet pussy, drawing the moisture to her clit. Skillfully, he rubbed. Firmly. Softly. Circling. Stroking almost to her anus and back.

Tormenting her until she was panting with the engulfing need.

He spanked her again, harder, each blow a noisy slap against burning, stinging skin. Only she was so aroused the blows felt like hot caresses that zinged right to her clit and amped up her excitement as if he was playing with a rheostat.

"Zeeeee. Please." Her hips twisted. Lifted.

"All right, pet." Pushing her legs apart, he settled between them. His thighs were hot against hers as he pressed his cock against her.

Cheek against the mattress, she panted in anticipation. Everything down there throbbed. Waited.

He entered her with a teasing inch...and with a merciless thrust, impaled her on his cock.

She gasped at the exquisitely painful, breathtaking feeling of being filled so full. Of being taken. As she strained to accommodate him, her interior walls pulsed a protest around the intrusion.

"I have missed this." His voice was deeper than normal. Harsh.

"Whose fault is that? Sir."

"*Bad* submissive." Chuckling, he swatted her bottom in a stinging reprimand.

She yelped...and burst into giggles.

"You've been associating with Gabi too often," he murmured before gripping her hips and yanking her back onto his cock forcefully enough to make her gasp.

There he stayed, deep inside her, as he pulled her upright onto her knees and leaned her back against him. He held her in place with a hand on her groin and one on her throat. As his warm hand curved around her neck, the slight pressure increased her sense of vulnerability, holding her immobile. His thick cock pulsed inside her as his fingers danced across her pussy.

She lifted her arms to touch him, to entice him, to make him start thrusting. Something...

The hand around her neck curled an infinitesimal amount tighter in warning. "Don't move, little one. Not at all." The finger circling her clit never slowed.

Deep inside her, pressure coiled. Grew.

Oh God. Poised on an excruciating edge, she shook with the need to come.

He kept her there. With torturous slowness, he moved inside her even as he stroked her clit.

"Please," she whispered.

"No."

Mercilessly, he continued until her muscles were drawn taut, her nerves screamed, her insides clenched around him.

"Yes, that's very nice." Slowly, he pulled out almost all the way. And stopped. Stopped everything. With a steely grip on her throat, on her pelvis, he held her caged as she whimpered and shook with desperate need.

Somehow, everything inside her gathered even tighter.

Suddenly, his fingers slid and circled the very top of her clit. With one driving thrust, he buried his length.

"Oh, *God*." A quaking sensation rippled deep inside her, increasing more and more, until it burst outward in rippling waves of exquisite pleasure.

"Mmm." His voice was a pleased rumble in her ear as he bent her forward until her cheek pressed against the mattress. Her butt stayed up in the air.

His hands closed on her hips, and he claimed her with merciless, pounding thrusts.

Another climax rolled over her. Mind-shattering pleasure engulfed her, consumed her.

He was deep inside her when his body went taut with the hot spill of his own release.

Still inside her, he rolled them both onto their sides. Cheek against her hair, he whispered, "I love you, Jessica."

As he wrapped her tighter in his arms, she glowed with the bone-deep satisfaction of wonderful sex.

And being loved.

CHAPTER EIGHT

Over the last hour, the hotel lounge that Zachary had rented for Mako's wake had grown crowded. A gratifying number of military personnel, NCOs and officers, had stayed for the send-off. Toasts and speeches had been given. Stories had been shared. The formalities were over, but no one was hurrying to leave.

The private lounge was a comfortable place to spend an evening, Zachary thought. Smaller than the public cocktail lounge, the room resembled an Alaskan fishing lodge with dark beams, hardwood flooring, antler chandeliers, and carved wood and leather furniture. Behind the mahogany bar, bottles of spirits alternated with trophy fish mounts. Across from the bar, a river rock fireplace with a rough-hewn mantel had a crackling fire. Guests had drawn near to bask in its warmth.

No matter how comfortable the setting, he'd rather be in his suite, talking and making love to Jessica again.

He was proud of her for braving his displeasure. For confronting him. And when he'd explained the trap for Weiss tomorrow, even though her face had gone pale, her voice was steady when she agreed a controlled setting would be safer.

His Jessica was quite a woman.

Earlier, he'd left her curled in bed, fragrantly warm and satisfied. Even as she insisted she'd attend the reception to support him, she'd fallen asleep. Lack of sleep, worry, pregnancy, and good sex had wiped her out.

Smiling at the memory, he stopped by the bar to pick up a Glenlivet scotch, then continued through the lounge, checking that the hotel staff were on the job, and making introductions as needed to ensure the guests were mixing.

In one corner, Bull was talking to a couple of generals who had good tales of when Mako'd been their drill sergeant.

Near the center of the room, Cazador was being entertained by officers who'd had Mako as their first sergeant.

Zachary smiled. No matter the rank, some sergeants were unforgettable, epitomizing everything the military stood for. He regretted not knowing Mako before he'd left the service.

At the door, deVries and a hotel security guard barred entry until guests were checked against Weiss's photo to ensure the lounge remained a no-shoot zone. DeVries had closed the window drapes, and made sure the door from the deck wouldn't open from the outside. He'd even put a sign on the door: PLEASE USE LOBBY DOOR TO EXIT.

Zachary had to admit it was a relief to let his guard down for a while.

As he crossed the room, he noticed Mako's oldest son had finally taken one of the oversized leather chairs. Bull and Cazador had been giving their brother increasingly worried looks.

The man looked up and gave Zachary a half-smile. "Any more run-ins with your sniper?"

"Let's hope he's smart enough to avoid rooms filled with military personnel." Zachary eyed him. "Gabriel, are you even supposed to be out of the hospital?"

"I'm not much for staying where someone puts me."

Zachary frowned. This son had gone into a mercenary outfit and had recently been in combat. Despite obviously being in pain,

Gabriel had the hypervigilant and deadly air of someone still at war. "Cazador said you were wounded?"

"A bit. Got me in the shoulder and hip." Gabriel waved a hand at the couch across from him. "Join me if you want."

Zachary took in the drink in Gabriel's hand, the pain lines on his face, and the haunted gaze—and he sat down. "I hope you're not adding alcohol to pain medication."

A corner of Gabriel's mouth drew up. "No, Doc. My last pain pill was at noon. I wanted to be able to drink my ass off, if needed."

"Good enough." Zachary studied him for a moment. Along with the pain was evidence of a lack of sleep. Grief for Mako... along with...guilt?

Gabriel motioned with his drink. "Your bodyguard mentioned your wife is here. Did I know you were married?"

"Not only married, but we have a daughter. She's one and a half."

Some of the lines on Gabriel's face disappeared with his smile. "Approaching the terrible twos?"

"God help us." Zachary missed the imp more than he could express. "She can make you want to strangle her one moment and melt your heart the next. I wouldn't—"

"Look at this." A striking redhead in a form-fitting blue dress stopped beside their sitting area. Her voice dropped to a sultry purr. "Here are two good-looking men sitting all by themselves. Alaska women should be ashamed."

Zachary eyed her. She didn't appear to be military, didn't look like one of the guests, really. In fact, he'd bet she was traveling for business and had gotten into the reception on the arm of one of the soldiers.

As she started to sit down, Gabriel's irritated shake of the head halted her. "Our Alaska women can tell when a man is hunting and when he's not. Sorry, miss, but we're not."

"Well, then." Ignoring Gabriel, she ran an interested gaze over Zachary. "I'll be at the bar if you change your mind."

Zachary watched her sashay away. "With that refusal to admit defeat, she probably does quite well in life."

"Maybe. Although it's irritating as hell." Gabriel lifted his beer. "A belated congratulations on your marriage and child."

"Thank you." Zachary sipped his drink, enjoying the slow bloom of warmth and studying the man opposite him. Gabriel had been a reserved child. The adult was probably even more reticent. Nonetheless... "Can I ask how you got hurt? Mako said you and Hawk were with a mercenary outfit."

Gabriel eyed him. "The sarge didn't usually share that with people."

"We'd been friends a long time." Zachary smiled slightly. "In fact, I met him about three hours before he grabbed you four from the foster home."

"Really? I thought you were in the service together." Gabriel's gaze focused on Zachary. "Come to think of it, you're nowhere near old enough."

"When we met, he'd been out for a decade and was having trouble. I told him to find ways to be around people more." Zachary shook his head ruefully. "If I'd known he'd interpret that to mean he should kidnap four children, I might have rethought my advice."

Gabriel choked off a laugh. "*Kidnapping* is a harsh word. He did ask if we wanted to go with him."

"You were ten."

"Yeah, but streetwise. I figure that adds about a decade."

Opening his hand, Zachary conceded him the point.

"However, he did mention it was your fault he was saddled with four smug little shitheads who were more fucked-up than a left-handed football bat."

Zachary chuckled. "I haven't heard that term in years. Old drill sergeants have a way with words, don't they?"

"Yeah, he had a mouth on him when he wanted to mo-tee-vate us. But you know? Anytime I won a '*good job*' from him, I walked on air for a good twenty-four hours after." Gabriel lifted his glass. "Absent friends."

Zachary clinked his glass against Gabriel's and took a swallow against the thick grief in his throat.

A burst of laughter from the bar quieted the room, then people resumed their conversations.

"Mako trusted me with his secrets." Zachary waited long enough for Gabriel to process that. "Tell me how you got hurt."

Silence.

"You were usually going from job to job in South America, I know. A mission went bad?"

Dark brows pulled together, and Gabriel sighed. "Fuck, you're stubborn."

He had no idea.

"Fine. A CEO was on a factory inspection. My squad—I was in command—was ordered to guard him." Gabriel looked away.

"I'm guessing someone shot at him, and you took the hit?" But that wouldn't leave the jarring mess of emotions Zachary could sense. "Who else got hurt?"

Gabriel was caught in the memory, his gaze unfocused. "It was a clusterfuck. No one told us the bastard had pissed off the factory—hell, the town. We got ambushed."

A town? Tensing inside, Zachary noted quietly, "A squad versus a town is impossible odds."

"No lie. I lost everyone but me and another teammate." Bitterness infused every word.

Too much bitterness. He'd called the client a bastard. "There's more to it..."

Silence.

Gabriel took a long drink of his beer. "Turns out we protected a worthless motherfucker I wouldn't waste my spit on, let alone the lives of my men."

"Ah." That kind of bitterness, Zachary understood. "You didn't know before you arrived that the civilians were angry?"

"No." Gabriel's mouth twisted. "We should have been told. Damned REMFs."

Rear-echelon-mother-fuckers. One of Mako's favorite expressions. Zachary hesitated. "Your assignment survived when your men didn't?"

"Not...exactly."

"I see." The withdrawn expression conveyed pursuing that question would be a mistake. "Are you still working for the merc outfit?"

"Not a chance. I'm done. If I'd known..."

If Gabriel had been warned about the town's animosity, he'd have been prepared, and his men might have survived. Mako'd said his oldest son was not only a master strategist, but that anyone he commanded would follow him into hell and back. A man didn't gain such loyalty without giving it back.

Guilt and grief were hard emotions to overcome.

"If you know all this, you know that none of it was your fault," Zachary said firmly.

Gabriel stared at the fireplace where the flames had died down to gleaming coals. He shrugged.

Zachary sat back. Yes, the man knew—and the knowledge hadn't made a dent in what his emotions told him. This wasn't the time to dig deeper, to try to help, and wouldn't be for a while to come. "Have you plans for what comes next? After you heal?"

"I'm going to go live in Mako's old cabin."

Zachary frowned. That log cabin in the middle of nowhere had no electricity, no plumbing, no running water, no phone service. "Why not your cabin in Rescue?"

Although all the sons had built cabins on the big Rescue property, none had ever moved there. They'd only used their homes like vacation cabins when visiting Mako.

"Too many people around. I want quiet."

Gabriel wanted an isolated place during a frozen Alaska winter where it only got light for a handful of hours. "You're not in any shape—"

"Why is someone shooting at you, Grayson?"

Excellent sidestep. Zachary almost laughed. Prying in return was fair play. "When I met a Marine who was psychologically unstable, I warned his senior officers to check on him. They did, and he blames me that he couldn't return to combat. He took a shot at me in Tampa too."

Gabriel blinked, then grinned. "And I thought my life sucked. At least I don't have a pissed-off Marine on my ass. One that's, at best, a mediocre shot."

"Let's hope *the third time's the charm* doesn't work for him."

"Let's hope." Gabriel's brows drew together. "What the fuck were you thinking letting your wife come here?"

"She was to stay in Tampa with our daughter." Zachary sighed. "But she could tell I was unhappy about something."

"About something?" Gabriel stared. "As in you didn't tell her someone wants to blow your head off?"

"A mistake on my part. She knows now." Zachary gave a rueful shake of his head. "She didn't take it well."

Gabriel broke out laughing. "I know it's not funny, but she sounds like a hell of a woman."

"She is." And much, much more.

"Good enough." Gabriel's gaze focused over Zachary's shoulder. "By the way, it took me a while to remember, but I've run into your bodyguard before. Iceman, right?"

The mercenary nickname had been mentioned in deVries's file. "DeVries, but yes, I believe Iceman was his handle." Back when the man had been doing contract work for a mercenary unit.

"He has a great rep. Good choice."

"Yo, Gabe." The bass voice came from across the room.

Gabriel looked around and raised a hand in acknowledgment.

"Seems Bull has someone he wants me to meet. If you'll excuse me?"

"Certainly."

"By the way, thank you for arranging the send-off. It's been good to remember the sarge as he was back in the day." Finishing off his beer, Gabriel struggled to his feet.

Zachary started to rise to help, caught the scowl, and sat back down. Mako hadn't accepted help easily. The apples hadn't fallen far from the tree.

Leaning on his cane, Gabriel headed toward his brother. In pain, grieving, haunted by memories and guilt. And alone.

Zachary shook his head, reminded of how blessed he was by having Jessica in his life. His two sons. Sophia. And a new miracle waiting to be born. He was rich in all that counted.

A few minutes later, drink finished, he set the glass down on the coffee table. Time to make another circuit.

"I see you lost your friend. Perhaps another would do?" The redhead from before sat down close enough he could feel her body heat and smell her musky perfume.

She really didn't take a hint.

"No. I'm married and—"

"I don't mind." She put her hand over his. "It's a shame to spend a night alone."

Being a mostly obedient submissive, Jessica had called Z to tell him she was on her way to the reception.

Aaaand, he told her she wouldn't be roaming the hotel by herself. If he couldn't, she couldn't.

So she was waiting in the room for some man to show up and escort her. She blew out a breath. Fair enough. Now she knew what was going on, she could understand Z's worry. And didn't want to add to it. She'd made him promise to be equally careful.

Someone is trying to kill him. Every time she thought of it, fear shuddered through her. But at least she knew and could add another set of eyes. Z had been wrong not to tell her at once.

A tap on the door made her jump. As her heart hammered crazily, she laughed at herself and checked the peephole. Z had described her escort as massive with a shaved scalp and black goatee.

Check, check, check. She opened the door. Whew, the description didn't do the man justice. He looked like the wrestler known as The Rock, for heaven's sake.

He grinned at her. "Hi, Jessica. I'm Bull Peleki, here to provide escort service."

"I'm all ready." She stepped out, pulled the door shut, and shivered slightly. Alaska was so *cold*, even in the hotel. She couldn't even imagine what it was like in the winter.

Walking beside Bull down the long corridor, she eyed him. Black pants, black shirt, black sport jacket. It was open and gave her glimpses of a shoulder-holstered handgun.

Huh. She'd thought Z's bodyguard was the mean-looking one who'd followed them to the suite earlier. "Are you Z's regular security guard?"

"No, that'd be deVries." The man smiled down at her. "Grayson was going to come and get you, but the bodyguard said no. He didn't want to risk the stalker getting into the reception. Since I happen to be armed, I volunteered."

"Oh." She frowned. He was carrying a pistol...for fun? "Well, I appreciate the escort."

"My pleasure. I'll admit, when Grayson said his wife had arrived, we hoped to meet you."

This wasn't fair. The man knew more about her than she did about him. "We?"

"My brothers and I. We're Mako's sons."

A wave of sympathy swept over her. "I'm so sorry for your

loss, Bull. I never met him, but from what Z said, he was an amazing person."

"Yeah. A total hardass ex-sergeant. Batshit crazy. And one of the most generous men ever born." He blinked a few times before smiling. "I have to say your husband is a pretty good guy. Did he ever tell you about the first time he visited us?"

"No, he just said he'd flown up to Alaska to check on you now and then." She smiled up at Bull. "But Z has a habit of leaving off the interesting bits. Tell me."

The man's booming laugh filled the corridor. "First, where we lived was so far off the grid, you couldn't even see the grid. And it took a four wheeler or snow machine to get to the cabin. Needless to say, no one visited. Until this guy showed up one day."

She tilted her head, trying to imagine Z in that setting. And... yes, she could. Whatever he did, he did well. "So he showed up out of the blue. Did he scare you?"

"He'd ham radio'd Mako, but us boys had no clue he was coming. We didn't even realize he was there until... Well, we were fighting. Back then, Hawk had days where almost anything would set him off." Bull shrugged. "He'd had shit happen before Mako got us."

Shit happened. To a child. Abuse of some sort. Jessica bit her lip, reminding herself that Mako's sons were grown now. Doing all right.

"Anyway, when he was in a mood, he'd start fights with whoever opened his mouth. That day it was Caz. I jumped in to break it up, but Hawk whacked me with a stick, and I lost my temper and started pounding him. Caz had pulled a knife—his first resort is always a knife. Gabe heard us and..." Bull laughed under his breath. "Gabe was born to be a cop, you know? He was trying to break up the fight."

Four boys, all fighting. A stick, knives, and fists. "That sounds horrible."

"Eh, it was getting ugly, and then this man was there. Shoved

Gabe off to one side. I tried to punch him, and he caught my wrist, yanked, and tossed me halfway across the clearing. Plucked the knife right out of Caz's hand and threw the knife as if he was playing darts. Lodged in a tree trunk. And then he picked Hawk up by the collar and just held him there while he talked."

Action, followed by psychology. Yes, that would be her Z. "Did the talking work?"

"Yeah." At the elevators, Bull pressed the down button. "And once Hawk stopped trying to fight, Grayson told us to tell Mako he was there, and he took Hawk for a walk."

"Oh boy, one of Z's chats?"

Bull grinned, knowing exactly what she meant. "Yeah, we all got those chats off and on over the years. But, you know, after this first visit, Hawk started to get a handle on his off days. And Grayson gave Mako—and us—a few clues on how to help."

Because that was what Z did. "I see."

"You got quite a man there."

"Yes, I do." Keeping up with him was the problem.

As the floors flashed past, she frowned at her reflection in the mirrored elevator walls. She still couldn't believe she'd fallen asleep. *Way to be supportive of your man, Jessica.*

And her exhaustion had given Z the exact wrong impression. With a sigh, she rubbed her hand over her stomach. *We have to do better than this, baby.*

"You look gorgeous." Bull had obviously noticed her studying herself.

He probably just liked the dress. It made her eyes greener—and although the velvety-soft dress was modest, she had more than ample cleavage no matter what she wore.

"Thank you, but I was trying for healthy and strong, rather than pretty." She'd nailed the healthy part, at least. She'd straightened her wavy long hair to a smooth, shining fall of golden blonde, and the salon had added pale streaks that brightened her coloring. She'd taken time to put on makeup so Z would notice her eyes—rather than the dark circles beneath. A dusting of blush certainly hadn't hurt.

"Strong and healthy?" His black eyes took on a thoughtful look.

She shrugged. "He goes over-the-top trying to protect me. Because that's who he is—but it isn't who we are together. Sometimes he forgets that."

Bull blinked. "That sounded like gibberish, but somehow it actually made sense."

Laughing, she walked with him out of the elevator, past the busy cocktail lounge, across the lobby, and to the private bar. A placard announced: *Michael Tyne: Send-off Wake*. Two men blocked the entrance.

One of the men at the door was the bodyguard—the man Z had tried to draft into taking her to the airport. She still couldn't believe he'd refused Master Z.

Blond with military-short hair, he wore black jeans and a black T-shirt over a thickly muscled chest. His square jaw looked stubborn, and his gray-green eyes were scary sharp.

But the man worked for Simon, and if he was guarding her husband, then the scarier the better.

He nodded at Bull, then his gaze came to her.

She smiled. "Good evening. Mr. deVries, right?"

"Just deVries." His voice was as gravelly rough as Master Sam's, his expression unreadable.

"Got it. I'm Jessica."

Unimpressed, he scanned the lobby behind her, left and right, before his gaze returned to her. "Your husband is inside. Go on in."

And stop interfering with his job. *Okay, then.*

"Thank you." Followed by Bull, she walked into the room. Z sure knew some interesting people.

An older man standing with a group called to Bull. "Peleki, we have a question for you to resolve."

Bull paused and shook his head at the man. "I need to—"

She patted his arm. "You escorted me here where it's safe. I can handle finding Z."

When he hesitated, she laughed "Seriously." And moved away before he could argue further.

Stubborn over-protective men. God love them.

The room was crowded with guests. Mostly male, although there were couples here and there. Some wore dress uniforms; some were in civvies. Almost all of them possessed that air of someone who'd been to war.

Z had said he put out the word over the military grapevine, and soldiers had shown up from everywhere to honor the first sergeant.

As she walked across the room, she overheard comments that said Mako had taught a generation of soldiers how to serve with honor. How to stay alive. How to work as a team. She wished she could have met him.

After wandering around, she reached the back of the room and finally spotted Z.

With a woman.

Jessica let out an exasperated breath. Honestly. It wasn't his fault; sheesh, he didn't even flirt. And yet, the man attracted women like a lightbulb attracted moths.

Time to shoo away another bug.

She listened long enough to ensure she wasn't interrupting anything except a woman on the make. Who wasn't picking up the clues.

So without so much as a *may I, Sir* or an *excuse me, please,* she plopped herself right onto Z's lap.

She felt his surprise, then his silent laugh. Closing his arms around her, he drew her up against his hard chest.

Acting as if she was sitting on a chair rather than a man, Jessica smiled at the redhead. "Hi there. I'm Jessica. How did you know the sergeant?"

The woman blinked. Frowned. "I didn't have the pleasure of meeting him. I, uh, came in with a guest, but..."

But she'd seen Z, right?

The woman's gaze slid over Z, and Jessica knew what she was admiring. A man with hard, chiseled features. Clean-shaven. Immaculate. Tailored black pants and silky black shirt. Treacherously elegant.

"I see." And Jessica did. Z's appeal couldn't be denied.

"It was nice meeting you, Jessica," the woman said. "I need to be going."

As the woman walked away, Z rubbed his cheek against Jessica's. "I did tell her I was married."

"I'm sure you did." Jessica caught his face between her hands the way Sophia liked to do and smiled at him. "You are just too gorgeous for mortal women to resist."

"Mmm." He kissed her lightly. "And you are just too—"

"Well, that was fun to watch." Choosing a leather chair across from them, a man sat down with a pained breath. Tall and muscular. Thick dark brown hair, much too long for the military. Sharp, dark blue eyes. After leaning his cane against the coffee table, he smiled at Jessica. "I'm Gabe MacNair. That was a strategically effective defense of your property. I wish I had someone who'd take up arms for me."

"I don't know if I'd consider Z my property." More the opposite in the BDSM world, right?

"You should." Z lifted her hand, kissed it, and turned it over to show her wedding ring. "I am yours as much as you are mine." His finger ran over her diamond choker, the one he'd fastened around her neck on their wedding day. The symbol of her submission to him. His voice deepened to a resonant growl. "And you are *mine*, kitten."

Unable to resist—she'd never been able to resist him—she kissed his cheek, his chin, and melted against him as he took her lips in a quick, but most possessive kiss.

When he let her go, she curled an arm around his neck and leaned against his chest. Face it, she loved sitting on his lap.

"Did you get enough sleep?" Z studied her face, then his gaze swept over her and his eyes narrowed. "Well, now... Stand up for a minute."

His firm hands around her waist steadied her—*damn high heels* —and she stood in front of him. Blushing.

He leaned back, smiled, and made a circling motion with his finger.

As she turned slowly, the masculine appreciation in his expression made every moment of preparation worth it. "You look stunning, little one."

"Thank you." When she sat down—beside him this time—he wrapped an arm around her, pulling her closer. He was so warm, and every breath brought her the light citrus scent of his aftershave.

And, oops, they weren't alone. Blushing, she looked at Gabe. "Sorry. New dress."

"It's a great dress." Gabe had a nice smile, but she could see the way he moved carefully, the tight lines of pain around his eyes.

"Are you all right? Can I get you something—alcohol? Aspirin?" She winced, realizing the question might not be the most tactful.

"I've been remiss," Z said. "Jessica, this is Gabriel, one of Mako's sons. He ran afoul of some weapons-fire and just got out of the hospital today. Gabriel, this is my wife, Jessica."

Gabe nodded to Jessica. "Good to meet you. And I'm all right —just sore."

Weapons-fire. What a polite way of saying someone shot him. Her stomach tightened. First Z, now Gabe. What was wrong with the world?

"I see you found your man." Bull dropped down in one of the chairs.

"Thank you for the escort, Bull," Z said.

"My pleasure completely." Bull looked up and grinned at an approaching man. "And here's Caz. Caz, this is the Jessica we wanted to meet."

"Jessica, it's a pleasure to meet Zachary's wife. I'm Cazador Ramirez, another brother." Graceful as a dancer, the other man leaned forward to shake her hand. Dark eyes, dark hair, brown skin, and a sinfully smooth voice with a touch of a Spanish accent. The man was probably deadly when it came to women.

Had Mako chosen the best-looking kids in that foster home to adopt?

"Cazador. Hi."

CHAPTER NINE

Listening to his brothers talk with Grayson and his pretty wife, Gabe leaned back against the soft leather cushions of the couch and tried to ignore the growing ache in his hip and shoulder. Beer hadn't proven nearly as effective as pain medication. But damned if he'd leave yet.

Over the evening, he'd met the people who'd come to honor Mako, heard their stories, and shared a few of his own. It'd eased the grief inside him. Some.

Telling Grayson about the ambush, losing his men, and the company's betrayal had been an odd sort of relief. The man's response, *"If you know all this, you know that none of it was your fault,"* also helped. Grayson wasn't a green civilian. He'd been Special Forces and knew the fucked-up shit that happened in combat. He'd said it like it was.

Gabe sighed. He was a fucking mess. He needed to be alone to deal. Solitude worked for him—and Hawk, too. Caz and Bull preferred to talk. *Dumbasses.*

"You were going to tell us more about your shooter," Bull said to Grayson.

"Yes, I owe you that." As Grayson explained who the sniper

was, Gabe watched the little blonde edge closer to her husband. Her face was calm, but her body language shouted that she was terrified for her man.

Gabe was pleased for him. Although a couple of serious relationships and a failed marriage had taught Gabe he wasn't a good bet, he had to suppress a twinge of envy for someone who'd made it work. For someone who had a mate looking at him with such obvious love.

"What's been done to catch this guy?" Gabe asked.

"The police in Tampa have a warrant out for his arrest. They—and a private investigation company—are monitoring Weiss's family and friends in case he makes contact." Grayson sighed. "He hasn't used his credit cards, probably because he emptied his bank account."

"What skills are we looking at?" Caz asked.

"His physical fitness is excellent. Expert with a rifle—he wanted into the Marine Scout Sniper program." When Jessica shivered, Grayson pulled her onto his lap. "However, I doubt he'd have passed the psych evaluation."

"Yeah, guess not." Bull frowned. "He's here now. Has the APD gotten a heads-up?"

"Yes. The police received the files as well as the latest photos," Grayson said.

"Are you planning to just wait around and—" His gaze on Jessica's white face, Gabe decided not to finish that question.

Grayson's lips quirked. "No, I'm done with waiting. DeVries's security company has three operators coming in tonight. Tomorrow, we'll set up a trap with a limited field of fire. Since Weiss has poor impulse control, I doubt he'll resist."

"Sounds like a good plan." Gabe frowned. "You must have a photo of him."

"Of course." Grayson pulled out his cell and selected a photo. "I should have shown you this earlier, Jessica."

Jessica accepted the phone and studied it before passing it to Gabe.

Weiss had deep-set brown eyes beneath a pronounced brow ridge, fair skin, and sandy hair in a high and tight cut. He'd stand out anywhere except on a military base. "Height and build?"

"Five eleven. Muscular, bulky build." Grayson took the phone back.

"We'll keep watch." Bull smiled at Jessica whose face was still pale. "Are you two going to be in Anchorage awhile? I'd enjoy guesting you at my brewery and restaurant."

"That sounds wonderful, but I'm not sure how long we're staying." When she turned those big green eyes on her husband, Gabe had to smile. He didn't know how any man could turn her down, no matter what she asked for.

Grayson ran a finger down her cheek and smiled at Bull. "We'd love to come by. Bull's Moose Restaurant, correct?"

Bull's booming laugh rang through the room. "I take it the sarge mentioned it?"

"He was very proud of you." Grayson glanced at Caz and Gabe. "Of you all. But he did mention how much he liked taste testing and helping pick which brews made the Bull's seasonal list."

"Did he?" Bull's smile was wide, although his eyes had reddened.

"I thought he lived in a cabin in the middle of nowhere," Jessica said. "How did you get beer out there?"

"Mako moved to Rescue near Kenai Lake a few years ago," Gabe said.

Brows together, she glanced around the room, obviously confused as to why the send-off was in Anchorage, rather than Rescue.

"I'm not sure more than one or two of the townspeople ever met him," Bull answered Jessica's unasked question.

"That'd be about right." Gabe snorted. "The sarge might've moved close to town, but he stayed a suspicious old survivalist."

He doubted the pretty woman had any idea how that kind of paranoia affected a man's life—let alone the children he raised. But Grayson's steady gaze held understanding.

The doc shook his head. "When we talked, he told me he'd hired a lawyer to put his affairs in order."

"Surprised us, too," Caz said. "Apparently Mako stuck in some time-contingent clause that the lawyer can't even discuss until spring."

"Trust the sarge to come up with some odd shit," Gabe said. "Probably obscure directions to a weapons cache, right?"

Bull laughed. "You're thinking of when he hid our clothes?"

Seeing Jessica's puzzled expression, Caz explained. "We'd been skinny-dipping, and he stole our clothes and stashed them all over the forest, then handed us notes with compass directions to each spot."

Jessica's mouth dropped open. "A naked treasure hunt?"

"He left us our boots." Gabe exchanged grins with his brothers.

"Gotta say," Bull added, "being bare-ass naked and running through the wilderness to beat an approaching rainstorm has its moments."

Grayson was suppressing a smile, but his wife looked horrified. "Oh my God, seriously? How old were you?"

Bull considered, glancing at Caz. "I remember half your curses were almost understandable, so you were speaking pretty good English by then. I guess I was about ten? Gabe would've been eleven."

The outraged sputters coming from Grayson's wife were cute.

"It's all right, Blondie," Gabe told her. "We managed all right. Although there was one T-shirt I never did find."

"You knew Mako was like that, and you left little children

there?" Jessica glared at her husband as if he should—and could—fix any problem in the world. *Lucky bastard.*

Grayson's mouth twitched. "Although I gave him my address when we met, he didn't reciprocate with his. I had no idea Mako had...appropriated...children until he wrote to me a year later."

"Yeah, that was the sarge," Caz said. "Paranoid to a fault."

"We exchanged letters sporadically since he only checked his PO box every couple of months and not at all in the winter. Eventually, he gave me directions to the cabin." Grayson's gaze met Gabe's. "I was honored by his trust."

Feeling his eyes sting, Gabe looked away.

"He was doing what he could, Jessica," Caz said. "I didn't realize it at the time, not till I had counseling classes in grad school. Then I realized we'd had our own intermittent counselor."

Gabe frowned. "What?"

"All those times he'd ask one of us to walk with him, show him something in the forest. He didn't talk much...mostly just listened."

Gabe frowned at Caz, then Grayson. Well, damn. That put a whole new meaning on those long walks. Of course, they hadn't realized he was a psychologist until years later. "You were checking if we were doing all right with him, weren't you?"

"Partly." Grayson moved his shoulders. "You all had a rough start to life. If you'd needed more help than Mako could provide, I wanted to know. To be able to intervene."

"Guess we passed your test." Bull was so obviously unworried that Gabe grinned. Not much ruffled the big guy.

"I'm sure you've had problems to work through since then, but yes." Grayson smiled. "Having someone in your corner, no matter the odds against you, can heal a remarkable amount of wrongs. Mako did well by you."

Yeah, you did, Sarge. Gabe swallowed hard. *Thanks.*

"Well." Bull cleared his throat. "There's a colonel over there who asked to be introduced to you, Grayson. Sounds like a friend was discharged and is having a hard time of it."

"Of course." Grayson hesitated and looked down at his wife. "Will you be all right here or—"

The colonel probably wanted to talk in private, Gabe guessed. He gave Grayson a look—*I'll guard your woman* before turning to her. "Why don't you let me buy you a drink, Jessica? I can keep the riffraff away until your man returns."

"That would be wonderful. Thank you." Her smile lit up her face.

Grayson gave him a grateful nod and followed Bull across the room.

To Gabe's left, Caz straightened, looking across the room. "Now there's a pretty *mamacita*."

Gabe followed his gaze. At the bar, the redhead who'd flirted with Grayson was in a group of male admirers. She wasn't a bad choice, at least for Caz who liked people, especially female people. Since he had the legendary dark Latin looks and charm, women liked him back. "Pretty, yes. But one of these days you're going to bed the wrong female."

"No, 'mano. I'm very careful and clear that we are only indulging in a few hours of fun. Nothing more."

"You keep telling yourself that. Jessica, let's go find drinks." Bracing his hands on the couch, Gabe tried to stand. Damn hip felt as if it had frozen in place. Some guard dog he'd prove to be.

Without being asked, Caz put a hand under his arm and pulled him up.

Dammit. Gabe shot him a glare.

His brother's attempt to smother a smile sucked. Then he added insult to injury by handing Gabe the fucking cane. Having excellent survival instincts, Caz also moved out of range.

"You're an overprotective bastard, you know," Gabe growled.

"Oh, Gabe, you should try being *married* to an overprotective bastard." Jessica rolled her eyes.

Gabe busted out in a laugh.

"If you will excuse me," Caz flashed a grin, "I have somewhere I need to be." He moved away, heading straight for the redhead.

"Idiot." Gabe turned to Jessica. "Time for alcohol."

"Definitely."

Limping, Gabe guided his charge to an unoccupied spot at the bar's far end, near the back door.

He'd been gratified to find that the hotel carried his brother's brand, and now, the bartender asked Gabe, "Another Bull's Off-the-Road?"

"That'd be good, thanks." Gabe looked at Jessica. "What's your pleasure?"

"A Sprite would be wonderful."

As the bartender moved away, Jessica looked around. "The room is clearing out. Looks like the evening is about over."

"It was a fine send-off. Your man did—"

"Let us in!" At the double doors, a large number of inebriated young men were trying to shove past the hotel staff and deVries.

One drunk managed to get past. Another also slipped by.

Gabe chuckled. With that many bodies trying to shove past, DeVries would have to either disable or knock out the young asses to stop them—but that'd be overkill.

A few more made it through.

"Are they going to be a problem?" Jessica put her hand on his arm.

Gabe gave the intruders a quick perusal to ensure the sniper wasn't in the group. "No, they're too young to be Weiss. They're probably with the academic convention going on."

The PFD—the dividend paid to Alaska residents—had just been dispersed. He'd bet a lot of them were drinking a portion of their funds this evening.

"Right, I saw the WELCOME signs. They do look like grad students, don't they?" She grinned as one did a victory dance across the room. "They sure act like students."

Having made it inside, another straggler was drunkenly shouting, "Where are the strippers?"

"Outside, you dumbass, they're outside on the deck," another yelled.

"Woohoo, naked women. The night is looking *up*."

Like a herd of caribou, the group stampeded through the private lounge to the rear of the room. Gabe pulled Jessica back to keep her from getting bumped.

At the back door, the drunks ignored the sign, flung open the door, and crowded out onto the unlit deck.

Dismayed shouts sounded.

"I don't see any strippers."

"There's nothing out here."

"What the fuck? That guy *said* there were lap dancers."

At the door to the lobby, deVries was arguing with a hotel manager, probably demanding that security evict the trespassers.

Gabe grinned as unhappy comments continued to drift back through the open deck door. No strippers were out there—only a cold, wet night.

What a crazy evening, Jessica thought. Whatever had made the idiots think there would be strippers outside in forty-degree weather? As the first disappointed young man trudged back inside, accompanied by a gust of frigid air, she snickered. "Aw, I guess the poor guys didn't find any naked women out there."

"Life is full of disappointments." Gabe paid for their drinks and grinned as more of the grumbling idiots returned. "Let's hope the lack of easy women is their worst letdown this year."

"Hey, here's a woman." One young man gave Jessica what he probably thought was an inviting leer.

Ew.

She'd learned talking to drunks rarely proved effective, so she simply turned away to face the bar. Unfortunately, sometimes even what her Regency novels termed the "cut direct" didn't work.

Like now.

The dumbass's voice rose. "Hey, I'm talking to you, woman."

"No." Gabe's deep voice held an edge that could cut. "You're *not* talking to her. Move on."

Jessica turned far enough to see the drunk backpedaling quickly. If he'd had a tail, it would have been between his legs. "You're very effective, Mr. MacNair."

He inclined his head, the laugh lines beside his eyes creasing. "Good to hear, Mrs. Grayson."

The remainder of the young drunks came inside, crowding the bar area.

"I'm sorry to be the bearer of bad news, but this is a private party." Z stood by the fireplace, one arm on the mantel. No anger sounded in his deep voice, just intimidating self-possession. "Please leave now."

Without even trying to protest, the young men started trudging toward the lobby door.

Gabe's lips quirked. "Your man is just as effective, if not more so."

"He has a talent." Even if not in the lifestyle, few people dared to argue with Master Z.

Smiling, she turned to admire her Dom.

A man blocked her view—one of the men who'd returned from the deck. He wasn't leaving. Oddly enough, this one didn't look drunk or like a grad student. His hair was buzz cut along the sides and...

It was *Weiss*.

He pulled a pistol from his waistband, pointing it at Z.

"No!" She lunged, hitting him right in the back, making him stagger. The handgun fired with a sharp *crack*.

"You bitch." Weiss spun, shoved her into the bar, and turned the pistol on her.

She froze, staring at the huge black barrel. His finger was on the trigger.

Gabe's cane whacked into Weiss's wrist, knocking his arm to one side.

Jessica felt the vibrations as the bullet hit the bar.

Reversing the cane, Gabe swung at Weiss's head.

Weiss dodged and darted full speed out the deck door.

Clinging to the bar top, Jessica frantically scanned the room. Had the bullet hit Z?

She spotted him as he dashed out the door after Weiss.

"No, *dammit*." She stared in disbelief.

Bull and Caz followed him.

At the lobby door, pistol pointing at the ceiling, deVries was brutally shoving through the crowd of drunks—the ones who must have inadvertently blocked him from shooting Weiss. He made it through and tore through the doorway after the others.

Jessica took two steps after them, and Gabe caught her around the waist. "Uh-uh, Blondie. We sit this one out."

"But—"

"I know. It'd be fun to play, but not this time."

To play? She stared at him incredulously. *Men.* Their brains really did get fried from all that testosterone.

Z was out there. Hunting a murderer in the night.

CHAPTER TEN

Zachary knew hunting an armed murderer in the dark was insane, but he wasn't about to turn back. Not when the sight of his tiny wife slamming into a murderer kept replaying in his head. How the man's pistol had swung toward her. If Gabriel hadn't intervened, Weiss would have killed her.

Jessica. She had the guts of a warrior. He wouldn't have her change, yet...he could so easily have lost her.

He'd not give Weiss another chance to hurt her.

Taking cover behind a tree, Zachary pulled the Glock from his ankle holster.

As sounds came from behind him, he half-turned.

A formless shape moved in the darkness, growing huge enough for him to identify the man. Bull.

Then another man silently slid through the wooded area. Moonlight gleamed off the blade in his hand. Cazador. Mako'd called him a natural hunter.

Dammit. He'd asked Mako's sons to help keep watch—not to be out here. Not to risk their lives.

More fool him. He should have known they wouldn't settle for being observers. Guilt swept through him. *I'm sorry, Mako.*

Shadows moved on the shoulder-high deck as deVries silently eased over the railing and disappeared into the darkness.

Zachary gritted his teeth. There were too many people in danger because of him. It was time to end this—and without getting any of his people killed.

A rustling came from ahead. A branch snapped. Weiss wasn't as quiet in the woods as Mako's sons were, and he was headed east.

East wasn't good. The hotel backed up to the Fish Creek greenway—a strip of dense forest and underbrush. Farther east, the greenway opened into large parks with even more cover for Weiss.

"Herd him toward the creek," Zachary said, just loud enough for Bull and deVries to hear.

A huff of breath came back as acknowledgement.

Zachary headed toward the rustling sound, detouring around underbrush, avoiding clear moonlit patches in case Weiss stopped running and started shooting. Stopping briefly, he shot several times at tree trunks he could see clearly, directing the fire to make Weiss veer right. Finished, he dove to the right behind a tree.

To the left, Bull fired several more shots, and deVries did the same.

Herding.

The rustling turned west. A moment later, the cracking sound of pistol fire split the night.

One bullet whizzed past Zachary, tearing through foliage. He fired at the muzzle flash, then to the left and right.

Even as he heard Weiss's pained grunt, Zachary ducked behind a tree.

A bullet *thunked* into the trunk. Weiss's return fire had almost caught him.

Zachary's mouth went dry. Ice and heat danced over his skin. Every sound was amplified. Memories flashed like photos as he dropped back into a war zone of years before.

Not. Now. Closing his eyes, he pulled in a breath and shook off the flashback. Tightening his grip on the Glock, he moved forward.

He'd hit Weiss. Was it enough to slow him down?

More shots were exchanged.

Using the available cover, Zachary headed right. With muzzle flashes revealing their positions and trees hindering the lines of fire, it was 50/50 whether Weiss or someone else would get lucky first.

He needed to get closer.

Under the cover of fire, Zachary silently moved toward Weiss.

Farther to the left came voices. A woman was speaking. "What's going on?"

Bull's voice rose. "Hold fire. We have civilians in the area."

Worse and worse.

The civilians were to the left. Zachary heard a rustling ahead and to his right. Quietly as possible, he trailed the sounds.

In the dappled moonlight, a crouched-over man darted through the brush, utilizing any available cover.

It was Weiss...probably. Or it could be some poor hiker fleeing an obvious war zone.

Zachary cursed silently. He couldn't take the chance.

Closer.

In the distance, sirens wailed, growing louder.

A branch snapped under his foot, the sound of breaking wood too loud. Even as Zachary dropped to the ground, a bullet thudded into the tree behind him.

More gunshots sounded as if Weiss was simply shooting blindly. In a circle.

A crash sounded. Someone had fallen.

Zachary's jaw clenched.

"Stand up, asshole," Weiss shouted at someone.

Zachary sprinted forward, stopping at the edge of a clearing. The moonlight illumined a nightmare.

Faced away from Zachary, Weiss held a gun on Bull who'd just risen to his feet. Blood streamed from Bull's leg.

Weiss gestured with his pistol. "You're gonna walk me out of here, you bastard. Tell your buddies to drop their weapons and come out where I can see them."

Zachary couldn't shoot Weiss in the back—the bullet would over-penetrate and hit Mako's son, too. Or Weiss's finger would spasm on the trigger with the same result.

Movement flickered on the other side of the clearing. DeVries. A glint of metal more to the right might be Cazador. But they'd have the same problem Zachary did.

Weiss must be made to point the pistol somewhere besides at Bull.

Jessica, if this ends badly, I'm sorry. Zachary stepped out from behind the tree. Into the open. "Ah, Mr. Weiss. What a surprise to find you here."

"You!" Weiss spun, his handgun whipping around to target Zachary.

With a meaty thud, a knife lodged in the Marine's back. His weapon fired.

Into the ground.

Staggering, he tried to lift his handgun—and another pistol cracked. The bullet struck Weiss in the temple. His knees buckled, and he dropped.

Surprised to be alive, Zachary let out a slow breath and bent down to check the man for a pulse. None.

Cazador shot a glare at the body before pulling another knife. He sliced through his own sleeve and ripped it off. Folding it, he pressed it against the bullet hole in Bull's leg.

"Ow, shit, Caz, that hurts."

"Oh, *pobrecito*."

Brothers. Zachary smiled slightly and glanced at the three men. "I don't have words enough to express my gratitude. But thank you all."

He got back nonchalant shrugs.

After helping Bull sit on the cold ground, Zachary took over holding the wound dressing. "Bull, I'm sorry. I didn't want—"

"Stuff it, Grayson." Bull stifled a groan as Cazador put pressure on the exit hole in the back of his thigh. "If the shot had busted my leg, I'd've been pissed, but this little bullet went through nice and pretty. I'm just glad Weiss wasn't using a .45."

"No shit," deVries muttered. "Now that would've been a mess." He glanced at Zachary. "Cops are headed this way. I'll lead them in."

When she'd heard the crackle of gunfire, Jessica had tried to run outside. Stupid, sure, but Z was out there.

Gabe had caught her around the waist and ruthlessly dragged her to a couch that faced the open deck door. After seating himself, he'd pulled her down and stretched his arm along the back cushion behind her. "We're going to wait here, Blondie. Don't even try to argue."

Figuring his injuries would slow him down, she'd attempted escape. The jerk had hold of her long hair. *Ow.*

So they waited.

Even as the police arrived, swarming the private lounge, the deck, and into the blackness beyond, the firing had stopped.

Please, God, let Z be all right. Please.

No more gunfire had sounded for five minutes now. An eternity. Her hands were clasped so tightly in her lap her fingers had gone numb.

Damn you, Z. Why did he have to charge after Weiss? Anger rose, over and over, and died each time, because that's who her Master was. He didn't want someone else to take the risks for him. It wouldn't have even occurred to him to step back.

Could a person love someone for a personality trait and hate it too?

"Breathe, Blondie." Gabe put his hand over hers. When she glanced up at him, his dark blue eyes held the calm of a man far too familiar with violence and death. "We'll know what happened in a few minutes. Hang in there."

Please, please, please.

Voices came from outside, growing louder, the conversations all mixed up.

Bull's subterranean bass. "Don't think he was aiming, just shooting blindly. I caught a stray round—and went down."

She felt Gabe's hand tighten.

The harsh rasp of deVries's voice. "Grayson stepped out to get his attention. The weapon fired."

Fired? *Fired?*

No! Jessica tried to leap to her feet. Gabe still held her hair—and her hand. "Wait, girl."

And finally, she heard Z's deep, resonant voice. "Caz threw a knife—"

Gabe muttered, "Of course he did."

"...a bullet in the head..." The thump of footsteps on the stairs and deck drowned Z's voice out.

But he was alive. *Alive.*

"Now you can go, Blondie." Gabe gave her hair a tug and released her.

She flew across the room, out the door, and past the first group of men. *There.* All she could see was Z—and she ran straight at him.

Knowing he'd catch her.

As his arms wrapped around her and he sighed and rubbed his cheek in her hair with a murmured, "Kitten," she knew he was all right.

They were all right—and so was her world.

CHAPTER ELEVEN

The next morning, Zachary visited the hotel staff offices to offer verbal and tangible thanks for their help with Mako's reception.

And the police and shoot-out. Not what any respectable hotel wanted on the premises.

Everyone had been quite understanding.

Crossing the lobby toward the elevators, he hesitated. He was in dire need of coffee. The brand available in the room wasn't what he'd call drinkable. Turning, he headed for the hotel restaurant.

Jessica had still been asleep when he left the room. No surprise. In many ways, it was easier to be the person in danger rather than the one waiting and worrying.

Of course, her need to sleep in this morning might be because *he'd* had an excess of adrenaline to burn off last night. She hadn't complained.

He smiled. She hadn't been able to. After he'd aroused her to loud pleading, the people in the room next door (not deVries) had pounded on the wall. Hearing them, his little subbie had smirked and said he'd better let her climax.

Instead, he'd gagged her and kept her on the brink until she was shaking with need.

After they'd both come, she'd sworn at him, first in English followed by Andrea's favorite Spanish insults.

She'd apparently forgotten he knew Spanish.

He'd obviously been slipping as a Dom and Master. So he let her sleep and woke her up a couple of hours later for her punishment. Five swats—in various places—for each insult.

Then he'd taken her hard.

The neighbors would undoubtedly request a new room today.

"Good morning. Will anyone be joining you today?" The perky hostess had a cheerful smile.

"Possibly."

"Very good. Follow me, please." The restaurant, decorated in rich greens and browns, was fragrant with the aromas of bacon and coffee. After texting Jessica so she'd know where he was, he followed the hostess into the sunny restaurant.

Gabriel was seated at a window table.

"Excuse me, miss. I see a friend over there." Zachary motioned.

"Of course." She veered to the table where Mako's oldest son sat.

"Good morning. May I join you?" Zachary started to smile and then frowned.

Gabriel's face was tight with pain. Dark circles ringed his eyes. "Sure. Have a seat." He pushed out a chair with his foot.

The hostess set out another place setting and the menu. "I'll be back with coffee."

"Thank you." Zachary took a seat. "How is Bull's leg?"

"It'll be fine. Nice and clean, right through the outside muscle. Caz took him home from the ER and intends to babysit the wound care."

Dammit, Bull had been hurt because of him. Even as guilt swept over Zachary, Gabe shook his head.

"You didn't push him out that door, Grayson. Even if you weren't a friend, Bull's not one to sit out a fight. We weren't raised that way."

"I suppose not." Zachary shook his head. "Nonetheless, I'm grateful. To all of you. Thank you."

Just as his brothers had, Gabe shrugged and changed the subject. "Were you there when the lieutenant talked to the grad students?"

"The ones who opened the deck door? No."

"Heh. Turns out Weiss had been in the cocktail lounge and said there were strippers outside on the deck. He gave himself an easy back way into the reception."

"Ah, I'd wondered about that. He was cleverer than expected." Zachary leaned back in his chair and studied Gabriel. "You don't look as if you had any sleep last night."

"Not much." Gabriel gave him a sardonic look. "After the police interviewed you and Jessica and you left, the lieutenant showed up with more questions."

Zachary straightened. An interruption last night would have been quite annoying. "I take it you fended him off for us?"

"Yeah. I knew him from my rookie days on the force, so he let me and the others fill him in rather than summon you back. You owe me, Grayson."

"Indeed. What would you deem to be adequate reparation?" As the hostess set down a steaming cup of coffee, Zachary murmured his thanks and took his first sip. Hot, black, and fragrant.

The day was looking up.

Even as Gabe considered what outrageous deed he might ask for, he spotted Grayson's pretty woman entering the restaurant.

Blonde hair dancing over her shoulders, spring-green eyes, gorgeously curvy. All good, but what caught a man's eyes was how her face brightened when she spotted her husband.

And how her lips were kiss-swollen, her cheeks beard-burned, and her expression radiated happiness. She looked like a woman who'd been taken well and often—and thoroughly satisfied.

Grayson followed his gaze. Rising, he held his hand out. "Good morning, kitten."

"Good morning, Ma...my husband. I see you've found a source for coffee."

"I did."

Gabe stood as she joined them and remained standing. "It was good to see you two, but I have a physical therapy appointment in half an hour." One he didn't want to miss, since he needed the therapist to recommend exercises for independent therapy. For an extended period. Like a winter of being snowed-in.

"Will we see you again?" Jessica's brows drew together.

Unlikely, since he'd already checked out. "Hard to say, Blondie. I'm staying with Caz for a few days before leaving for the cabin."

Grayson's mouth tightened with his disapproval. "Gabriel..."

"Sorry, Doc. It's my choice to make, idiotic or not. I've spent many a winter in that cabin." In quiet and isolation, because there was nothing he wanted right now more than a world with no people in it.

"I can't stop you." Grayson gave him a level look. "But if you're still holed up there after breakup next spring, I'll come and yank you out."

"Jesus, you're a stubborn bastard." Yet the ice around his heart melted some with the warmth of Grayson's concern. "You two take care of each other."

As he limped away, he heard Jessica say, "You gave him that stare that sends me to my knees...and he called you a bastard. The man has balls."

The shrink laughed, something Gabe hadn't often heard from him.

Good for you, Blondie. Grayson was a good man—and he had a fine woman to stand by him.

Gabe wasn't feeling envy, not really. He didn't want a woman, not when he hurt as if someone had tried to rip him apart with bullets.

Oh, right—they had.

As he walked into the lobby, he rubbed his shoulder. Felt like a wolf's fangs were digging into the joint.

Even if he wasn't hurting, he didn't want a woman. Didn't want anyone. Mako's cabin in the middle of the wilderness was calling to him like a homing beacon for a lost soul.

He needed to talk his brothers into helping him haul a winter's worth of supplies out to the cabin. That wouldn't be easy. Brothers were a pain in the ass.

And the finest gift in the world. *Thank you, Sarge.*

Zachary watched Gabriel limp into the lobby. He must be hurting badly.

"Will he be all right?" Jessica's brow furrowed.

"Of course." The answer was instinctual...and *wrong*. A lie.

Zachary wrapped his hand around hers. Her fingers were small. Delicate. *She* was small and delicate, and every instinct he had said to protect her. From everything.

Yet being smothered in the name of safety wasn't what she wanted. And it snubbed their agreed-upon boundaries. She wasn't his slave, after all. His title "Master" was derived from the Shadowlands, not their relationship. He was her Dom; however, he didn't want a 24/7 submissive—even though his dominance didn't necessarily stop at the bedroom door—and she didn't want to be one. She stood on her own two feet, and her strength of character was one of the reasons he loved her. Nevertheless, he'd slid into a typical Dominant habit—being overprotective to the detriment of the relationship.

Last night, when spotting Weiss, she hadn't hidden. She'd charged the man and saved Zachary's life.

He needed to rein in the protectiveness.

"Z? Why are you frowning if Gabe will be all right?"

Looking into her clear green eyes, Zachary gave her a rueful smile. "My answer was more optimistic than truthful. An off-the-grid cabin in the bush is a poor choice for someone not one hundred percent healthy. Even worse, he'll be snowed-in and alone for months. Isolation tends to exacerbate the kind of grief and guilt he's feeling right now."

She started to rise as if to run after Gabriel and stop him.

"No, little one. It's his choice, as he pointed out."

"I suppose it would be bad form to tie him up and sit on him?"

He laughed and realized anew how much he'd missed talking to her. Although he always listened when she complained about her day, he'd stopped discussing his own problems. Because he was trying to shield his overworked submissive. *Wrong, again.* She needed to be part of his life. And he needed her there.

His warm-hearted woman with her quirky sense of humor balanced his world in a way no one else ever had.

"Have I told you today how much I love you?" he asked softly.

She wrinkled her nose. "You might have said something in the early hours, which would be considered today, I guess. I was too busy dying of heart failure to take it in."

"Your heart *was* pounding as I recall." That'd been about when he'd started lightly swatting her pussy.

She glowered at him, and then huffed a laugh. "I should have remembered you speak Spanish."

"A painful mistake on your part, yes." Really, it was a wonder she was able to sit down at all today.

Lifting her hand, he kissed her fingers. "By the way, did you get the video of our daughter? Your mother sent it earlier this morning."

"A video?" Her eyes lit. "Can I see?"

Zachary pulled out his phone, opened the gallery, and handed it over.

Sitting on the floor in front of a tiny desk, Sophia was coloring. Next to her, ears pricked forward in interest, Galahad watched intently. Whenever the toddler looked away, the cat lifted a furry paw and knocked another crayon to the floor. When she finally realized all her crayons were gone, she looked around, spotted them on the floor, and burst into infectious giggles.

As Jessica did now.

Grinning, Zachary pocketed the phone. "It's obvious our daughter is doing quite well without us. How would you feel about staying another two days? You've never seen Alaska; we could play tourist."

Jessica gave a tiny bounce. "Really?"

"I can think of nothing I'd like better." He cupped her cheek and leaned over to take her lips gently before murmuring, "And no one with whom I'd rather spend the time."

Smiling, she rubbed her cheek against his. "I love you, Master Z."

She squirmed slightly and muttered, "But I need to stand up now. My bottom hurts, you sadist."

Laughing, he pulled her up. When he wrapped his arms around her, his entire world seemed to glow. "In case you've forgotten, kitten, that pretty bottom is mine."

He bent to kiss the pout off her lips and murmur, "As are you."

ALSO BY CHERISE SINCLAIR

ABOUT THE AUTHOR

Cherise Sinclair is a *New York Times* and *USA Today* bestselling author of emotional, suspenseful romance. She loves to match up devastatingly powerful males with heroines who can hold their own against the subtle—and not-so-subtle—alpha male pressure.

Fledglings having flown the nest, Cherise, her beloved husband, an eighty-pound lap-puppy, and one fussy feline live in the Pacific Northwest where nothing is cozier than a rainy day spent writing.

Made in the USA
Coppell, TX
15 September 2023

21602495R00075